Praise for *New York Times* bestselling author
KASEY MICHAELS

"Kasey Michaels aims for the heart
and never misses."
—*New York Times* bestselling author Nora Roberts

"Kasey Michaels creates characters who stick with
you long after her wonderful stories are told."
—*New York Times* bestselling author Kay Hooper

"If you want emotion, humor and characters you
can love, you want a story by Kasey Michaels."
—National bestselling author Joan Hohl

Praise for Mindy Neff

"Mindy Neff masterfully blends humor
with a romance that will melt your heart."
—*Romantic Times Magazine*

Praise for Mary Anne Wilson

"Mary Anne Wilson's...characters
make for a remarkable read."
—*Romantic Times Magazine*

Dear Reader,

Harlequin American Romance has rounded up the best romantic reading to help you celebrate Valentine's Day. Start off with the final installment in the MAITLAND MATERNITY: TRIPLETS, QUADS & QUINTS series. *The McCallum Quintuplets* is a special three-in-one volume featuring *New York Times* bestselling author Kasey Michaels, Mindy Neff and Mary Anne Wilson.

BILLION-DOLLAR BRADDOCKS, Karen Toller Whittenburg's new family-connected miniseries, premiers this month with *The C.E.O.'s Unplanned Proposal*. In this Cinderella story, a small-town waitress is swept into the Braddock world of wealth and power and puts eldest brother Adam Braddock's bachelor status to the test. Next, in Bonnie Gardner's *Sgt. Billy's Bride*, an air force controller is in desperate need of a fiancée to appease his beloved, ailing mother, so he asks a beautiful stranger to become his wife. Can love bloom and turn their pretend engagement into wedded bliss? Finally, we welcome another new author to the Harlequin American family. Sharon Swan makes her irresistible debut with *Cowboys and Cradles*.

Enjoy this month's offerings, and be sure to return next month when Harlequin American Romance launches a new cross-line continuity, THE CARRADIGNES: AMERICAN ROYALTY, with *The Improperly Pregnant Princess* by Jacqueline Diamond.

Wishing you happy reading,

Melissa Jeglinski
Associate Senior Editor
Harlequin American Romance

KASEY MICHAELS

MINDY NEFF

MARY ANNE WILSON

The McCallum Quintuplets

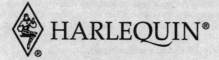

HARLEQUIN®

TORONTO • NEW YORK • LONDON
AMSTERDAM • PARIS • SYDNEY • HAMBURG
STOCKHOLM • ATHENS • TOKYO • MILAN • MADRID
PRAGUE • WARSAW • BUDAPEST • AUCKLAND

Special thanks and acknowledgment are given to
Kasey Michaels, Mindy Neff and Mary Anne Wilson
for their contribution to the
MAITLAND MATERNITY: TRIPLETS, QUADS & QUINTS series.

ISBN 0-373-16909-4

THE McCALLUM QUINTUPLETS

Copyright © 2002 by Harlequin Books S.A.

The publisher acknowledges the copyright holders
of the individual works as follows:

GREAT EXPECTATIONS
Copyright © 2002 by Harlequin Books S.A.

DELIVERED WITH A KISS
Copyright © 2002 by Harlequin Books S.A.

AND BABIES MAKE SEVEN
Copyright © 2002 by Harlequin Books S.A.

Visit us at www.eHarlequin.com

Printed in U.S.A.

CONTENTS

KASEY MICHAELS

is the *New York Times* and *USA Today* bestselling author of more than sixty books. She has won the Romance Writer of America RITA Award and the *Romantic Times* Career Achievement Award for her historical romances set in the Regency era, and also writes contemporary romances for Silhouette and Harlequin Books.

MINDY NEFF

published her first book with Harlequin American Romance in 1995. Since then, she has appeared regularly on the Waldenbooks' bestseller list and won numerous awards, including the National Readers' Choice Award and the *Romantic Times Magazine* Career Achievement Award, and was twice nominated for the prestigious RITA Award.

MARY ANNE WILSON

is a Canadian transplanted to Southern California, where she lives with her husband, three children and an assortment of animals. She knew she wanted to write romances when she found herself "rewriting" the great stories in literature, such as *A Tale of Two Cities*, to give them "happy endings." Over a ten-year career, she's published thirty romances, had her books on the bestseller lists, been nominated for Reviewer Choice Awards and received a Career Achievement Award in Romantic Suspense.

GREAT EXPECTATIONS
Kasey Michaels

Chapter One

The room was dark, the only light filtering through the slats in the vertical blinds on the single window overlooking Austin's Mayfair Avenue. The Texas sun wasn't all that strong at five on this March afternoon, but Dr. Madeline Sheppard still squinted slightly as she watched the illuminated screen in front of her.

The room was silent, the only sound the purring motor on the ultrasound machine pulled up next to the examination table where Maggie McCallum lay, also watching the screen on the ultrasound machine.

Madeline leaned a little closer to the screen, her lips moving silently.

"Dr. Sheppard?" Adam McCallum asked as he stood on the other side of the examining table holding his wife's hand, giving it a reassuring squeeze. "Is anything wrong?"

Madeline looked at Adam from overtop the tortoiseshell-framed half glasses she'd worn for close work since her thirty-fourth birthday, hoping she wouldn't be in bifocals for her thirty-fifth. She'd taken to attaching the glasses to a strap hung around her neck, although most times the glasses perched low on her nose because that was even easier than having them hang from the strap.

"Hmm?" she murmured, her mind still concentrated on the screen, what she was seeing on that screen. "Oh, I'm sorry, Mr. McCallum. No, no. Nothing's wrong. Quite the contrary. You just lie still a little longer, Maggie. I want to recheck something, that's all."

"Hey," Maggie said, laughing nervously, "take all the time you need. And I still don't know how you can see anything on that little screen."

"Oh," Madeline said, tongue in cheek, "I'm seeing something. Trust me, I'm seeing something."

She squirted a little more warmed gel on Maggie's belly and continued moving the sensor, watching the screen as, under her breath, she did a little arithmetic.

"Doctor, you're beginning to worry me, even if you keep saying everything's all right," Adam complained, walking around the bottom of the examination table to come peer over Madeline's shoulder as she used the small dials on the machine to box section after section of the screen, then repeatedly hit the Print button.

"Okay, all done," Madeline said, sighing as she lifted the sensor from Maggie's already faintly rounding belly, then wiped her patient's skin free of the lubricating gel. "How about you just zip up your slacks, and we'll go into my office, where we can all be more comfortable."

Before Adam, still hovering at her shoulder, could ask another question, Madeline grabbed the printouts and walked into the adjoining room. She shrugged out of her white examination coat, smoothed her loose-fitting, ankle-length dress and seated herself behind her desk. She folded her hands together on the small stack of printouts, took a deep breath and collected her thoughts.

The conversation she was about to have would be wonderful, at first. But then the questions would come, the fears would surface—all of them understandable, all of them possibilities that had to be addressed.

They came into her office holding hands, two good people. Good-looking, good hearts, good friends. Maggie, a schoolteacher and wife as well as an anxious, expectant mother. Adam, the son of Jackson McCallum who, providentially it would seem now, had financed this very building, the latest addition to the Maitland Maternity Clinic.

Officially, the new unit was called the Emily McCallum Multiple Birth Wing, in honor of the woman who had died thirty-one years ago giving birth to the McCallum triplets, Adam, Briana and Caleb.

Emily McCallum's delivery-room death would be very much on Adam's mind in a few moments, and Madeline mentally rehearsed how she would address those concerns.

How ironic that Adam and his wife had come to seek Madeline's advice as a fertility specialist several months ago. How wonderful that she had been able to help them. Now they would learn that the three of them were going to be a close-working team for the next seven months, along with Zachary Beaumont, the wing's highly qualified perinatologist, who specialized in high-risk pregnancies and multiple births.

Madeline watched them closely as the couple sat down in the leather chairs, still holding hands, both of them looking at her expectantly. Good word, expectantly. Because, boy, were these two ever *expecting!*

"Dr. Sheppard?" Maggie asked, her voice overly bright with nerves. "Are we right about the timing? I'm just two months along? Because I'm really having trouble with my waistbands, and I thought it would be too soon for that."

Adam laughed. "Maggie sees no relation between the chocolate-covered marshmallow Easter eggs she's discovered and her weight gain, Doctor. Me, I'm considering buying stock in the company, if their candies are really that good."

"Ha, ha," Maggie said, glaring at her husband for a moment, then smiling.

These two smiled at each other a lot lately. Madeline liked that; it made a nice change. Infertility strained many a marriage to the breaking point, and as both doctor and friend, she hadn't been unaware of the tension Maggie and Adam had been under through the months of fertility testing, the "come home, my temperature has gone up" pressure that took a lot of the romance out of any marriage.

But all that was over now. Maggie and Adam were pregnant. Now it was Madeline's job, and Zachary's job, to get Maggie to a healthy delivery.

"Okay," Madeline said, putting a smile on her face. "First, yes, Maggie, I'd say we're right on the money with your due date, especially since we've been routinely running pregnancy tests and monitoring your cycles. You're two months pregnant. Your uterus, however, is nearly twice the size of a two-months' gestation."

"It's twice as large *because*…?" Adam asked, leaning forward in his chair.

"Maybe because," Madeline suggested, "there could be more than one baby in there, Adam. We did discuss this possibility, remember?"

Maggie nodded. "Yes, we did. Adam was one of triplets, so that made us more likely to have a multiple pregnancy, even without the fertility drugs I took. You told us, Doctor. We knew the risks."

"And we told you it didn't matter. One baby, three

babies—we'd love them all,'' Adam added, his eyes going to the small stack of printouts Madeline had just picked up. ''We're having more than one? Is that what you're saying? Can you see them on there? I mean, really see them?'' He stood up, held out one hand. ''Let me see.''

Madeline deliberately put down the printout she'd been holding, folded her hands over the stack once more. ''In a moment. And, yes, Mr. McCallum, I can see them. I counted, counted several times, and there's no question. You and Maggie are going to become the parents of what we in the medical profession so ridiculously call multiples.''

Maggie gave a little cry and reached out to Adam, who held her close, kissed her hair, her cheek.

And Madeline watched, smiling with them…and waited for the other shoe to drop.

Adam was the first to sober, to look at Madeline, his eyes dark. ''How…how safe is this, Doctor? I mean it, be honest. My…my mother—''

''Your mother, Mr. McCallum,'' Madeline interrupted quickly, ''gave birth over thirty years ago, in a small-town hospital unequipped to handle her special circumstances. You know I've seen her medical records, and her complications, although still dangerous today, are much more manageable now. And, as we've also already discussed, the McCallum Wing is the most well-equipped, up-to-date facility in this entire region. We're going to take very good care of Maggie and your babies.''

''Babies,'' Maggie said, lightly pressing both hands against her belly. ''How many, Doctor? Two? Three?''

''They're still incredibly small, but I tried to capture them each separately.'' Madeline picked up the grainy printouts and began dealing them out in front of the expectant parents like playing cards, watching Maggie's and

Adam's eyes widening, their cheeks going pale. "One… two…three…four…and *five*."

Then she grabbed the ammonia packet from her top drawer and broke it under Adam's nose. Funny, it was usually the mother who fainted.…

"WE'RE GOING to have to pile pillows on the floor of the delivery room," Madeline joked as she ended her story about her newest expectant father. She sat low on her spine on the soft leather couch, her bare legs and feet propped on the glass-topped coffee table. "Otherwise, mother and babies will be fine, and Daddy will be admitted for a concussion. I mean it, Ian," she said, looking at her friend, who was looking at her bare feet, "the poor guy went out like a *light*."

Ian Russell picked up Madeline's crossed legs and slipped a section of the morning newspaper under them. "I'd do more than that," he said, heading to the small wet bar in the main living area of his spacious apartment to snag a bottle of soda from the refrigerator. "I think I'd be on the next fast jet to anywhere but here. Five babies at one time? Damn, Maddie, that's a litter." He held up a green plastic bottle, wiggled it. "Want one?"

"It is *not* a litter, Ian," Madeline replied testily. "And no, not that stuff. That stuff has no caffeine. I have about five medical journals to read tonight. I need caffeine. Lots of caffeine."

"Really? Sorry, all out," Ian said, grinning at her. "How about I spoon-feed you some of the coffee grounds left over from this morning? That ought to give you a kick start on staying up all night."

Madeline rolled her eyes, indicated with a wave of her hand that, yes, reluctantly, she'd take the soda he'd offered. "You don't really think multiples are litters, do you, Ian?'' she asked as he sat down next to her on the couch, rested his head against the back cushion.

"No, Maddie, I don't. But I get a real kick out of the way your nostrils sort of *flare* whenever anyone dares to say the word *litter* in your presence. Hell, I think you're doing a great job. Bringing happiness to previously infertile couples, bringing children into the world who will be loved, cherished—really wanted.'' He turned his head to look at her. "Okay? Am I forgiven?''

"I'll think about it, while you think about groveling. Because I absolutely love it when you grovel,'' Madeline said, raising the bottle to her lips, drinking deeply. Then she closed her eyes, tipped her head back and gave every indication of going to sleep.

Ian looked at her, shook his head. What a woman. She worked harder than any two men he knew, practically *lived* her job. No, her profession. What Maddie did, what she achieved, was a whole hell of a lot more than just a job. She had been this way, this dedicated, ever since he'd met her.

How long had he and Maddie known each other? Fifteen years? No, more like seventeen, ever since their freshman orientation class that first day at the university. Almost half a lifetime, considering they'd both turn thirty-five this year, Ian just two weeks after Maddie's birthday.

The Gruesome Twosome, that's what they'd called each other, a fairly uninventive name, but they'd liked it. He'd given her a little whirl, because that's what he liked—giving the ladies a little whirl—but it hadn't worked. She'd been too caught up in her studies to have much time for romance, and the one time he'd tried to kiss her, she'd laughed at him. Laughed!

But she'd been right. They were compatible. As friends, they were compatible. They'd even shared an off-campus apartment the last two semesters of school, Maddie doing the cooking, Ian the cleaning. And cleaning up after Maddie in the kitchen had been a full-time job.

Still, they were friends, great friends. Best friends. Nobody applauded louder when Maddie received yet another academic honor. No one laughed harder when Ian had to take to wearing dark sunglasses and a big hat to avoid the latest lady in his varied love life.

They'd gotten drunk together the night he learned that his father, from whom he'd been estranged for years, had died. They'd spent a month backpacking through Europe together before their last year of school. Maddie had cried on his shoulder when her first big love affair went belly-up, and he'd written her application for her internship.

And here they still were, not roommates anymore—Maddie lived in the apartment across the hall—but still best friends. She could tell him anything, and he'd listen, he'd understand. He could show up on her doorstep, feverish, hacking and sneezing, with a morning beard and bed hair, and she'd take him in, cluck over him, make him all better.

In fact, if they weren't such good friends, he'd marry her, except that marriage would probably just break up their friendship.

"Maddie?" he said, pushing a dark curl that had slipped onto her forehead, tucking it behind her ear.

"Hmm?" she said, her eyes still closed. "If you've got a hot date and you're asking me to move, you can just forget it. I'm staying right here."

"Long day, huh?"

"No more than most," she said, seemingly trying to open her eyes by raising her eyebrows—a fruitless exercise, to say the least. "But I had to tell one of my patients that the in-vitro didn't work. That was hard."

"Are you going to try again?"

"Uh-huh, thanks to the fund Jackson McCallum set up to help pay for the procedure for those who can't really afford the high fees." She finally succeeded in getting her eyes open, her deeply brown, wonderfully compassionate eyes. "I hate it that sometimes a couple's checkbook comes between them and the chance for a baby. It just doesn't seem fair."

"And she's off," Ian said, smiling. "I would have thought you'd be too tired to climb up on any of your many soapboxes tonight."

She wrinkled her nose at him. "When you're right, you're right. Topic closed. Now, do you want me out of here or not, because if you don't have a date I think ordering out for pizza sounds like a real plan. We rent a movie, pop some popcorn later? What do you say? Those darn journal articles can just wait for another day."

Ian winced. "Sorry, babe. Definitely a hot date." He pushed back his sleeve, looked at his wristwatch. "As a matter of fact, she'll be here any moment now, so if you wouldn't mind?" he ended, picking up her bare legs once more, pushing them off the coffee table so that Madeline had no choice but to get up. It was either that or slide onto the floor in a heap.

She gave her thick black mane a toss, then pulled at her extra-extra-large gray sweatshirt that all but hid the fact that she was also wearing a pair of cutoff jean shorts. Maddie had great legs, Ian knew, but that body of hers pretty much remained a mystery, even after all these years. He'd never met a woman so careful to conceal her body, mostly with goofy granny gowns or oversize sweats.

He stood up with her, flicked a finger against her shiny, makeup-free nose. Her naturally curly hair—and there was a lot of it—was still damp after her shower, and he liked the way it waved around her face. Such a change from the tight braid or the bun she usually squeezed it all into because she thought the scraped-back styles made her look professional. Professional, hell. Just as he'd told her about ten million times, in those granny gowns, with that hair, she looked like a gunnysack with bangs.

"Tomorrow night?" he asked her as he took her by the shoulders, turned her, aimed her toward the door. "Pizza, popcorn, the whole nine yards. My treat."

"You're on," Madeline told him, accepting the sneakers he picked up, held out to her. "Oh, no—wait. I can't. Dammit, Ian, I can't."

"Hot date?" he asked, a little surprised to feel a slight twinge somewhere inside him. A twinge? Of what? Certainly not jealousy. That would be ridiculous. Besides, if it was jealousy, it would only be because he enjoyed their movie nights so much. Maddie never missed a joke in the comedies, always guessed the murderer in mysteries and just about crawled inside him when they watched horror movies. And she made great popcorn. With cheese on it.

"No, silly. No hot date. Not even a lukewarm one, more's the pity. The girls are taking me out for my birthday."

"Your birthday? That's not for another two days. And besides, you're spending it with me, remember? Saturday night, you and me, reservations at Lone Star, two very thick, very rare steaks. You couldn't have forgotten?"

She reached up, kissed his cheek. "Relax, I haven't forgotten. How can I forget? You're paying the check. No, this is just a girls' night out, that's all. Just April, Annabelle and yours truly. We'll go to the mall straight from work, grab something to eat and do a little shopping."

"Really?" Ian said, looking at her, one eyebrow raised. "You're going shopping? At the mall? For *clothes?* And that would be voluntarily? I don't believe it."

"Very funny," Madeline said, heading for the door once more. "I'll have you know that I've agreed to let April and Annabelle pick out a new outfit for me. It's their birthday present to me, and I think it's a very nice gesture. Really." She wrinkled her nose. "Kind of. Sorta. Oh, how I'm going to *hate* this."

"Hold it right there, pal," Ian said, walking after her, grabbing her elbow as she reached for the doorknob. "There's got to be a story attached to this. Let's hear it."

Madeline pulled a face. "Man, you're a pain. Okay, okay, so there is a story. Sort of. I was speaking with a patient the other afternoon, out in the hallway of the unit, and the patient's little girl pointed at my stomach and asked when *my* baby would come out."

Ian's smile faded for two reasons. One, he knew Madeline's absolutely atrocious taste in clothes had caused the child's mistake—Omar the tent maker used less cloth—and two, he knew how badly Madeline wanted to be pregnant. Married and pregnant. Just pregnant, if she didn't marry soon.

He hated to hear her talk about becoming a single parent. She deserved so much more. She deserved a man who loved her, a family, even the requisite white picket fence around the family home.

He shook away his thoughts, tried to keep the conversation light. "When is the baby coming out? Ouch, babe, that had to hurt. What were you wearing? That green granny dress your mom sent you? I told you—"

"I know, I know. You've definitely told me. And, yes, the green granny dress my mom made for me, which is now residing in a charity bin outside the hospital. Anyway, Annabelle overheard the little girl, and the next thing I knew she and April had a conspiracy cooked up between them. Tomorrow night they're buying me a new outfit for my birthday. And they've told me I'd better come prepared with my plastic, because they fully intend to talk me into an entire new wardrobe. I'm going to hate every moment of this. Just *hate* it.''

"But you'll play nice?" Ian prodded. "You won't do what you did to me the last time I suggested you wear clothes at least *close* to your own size?"

"I didn't do anything to you, Ian, and you know it."

"Sure. Right," he agreed. "Now, what did you say again? I'm afraid my ears are still ringing. Wait—if I listen, listen closely, I can still hear it. 'Ian Russell, you can take that pitiful excuse for a dress and shove it straight—'''

He broke off as Madeline put down her head, as her shoulders sort of slumped. "Ah, hell, Maddie, I'm sorry. I didn't know that was such a sore spot with you."

Her head flew up, her chin jutting out. "It is *not* a sore spot with me, Ian. I just don't see the point. Do you know how many times a day I can be getting in and out of scrubs, my street clothes? It's just easier to dress as I do. Loose clothing, no buttons, no restrictions."

"No style, no glamour, no hairstyle, no makeup—okay, okay," he ended, putting up his hands as she growled at him. "I'm backing off, right now. But, man to woman, Mad, if you plan to go fishing, it's smart to put out a couple of lures."

Madeline opened her mouth, probably to tell him to close his, when there was a knock on the door. She grinned at him rather evilly. "Oh, gosh, your dress-up doll's here. Guess I'd better hit the road."

"Very funny," Ian said, heading toward the door.

"And Rosemary's not a toy. She's a software whiz. Very creative."

"I'll just bet she is," Madeline said as he opened the door. She breezed past Rosemary, who frowned at her, then smiled at Ian.

"Who was that?" Rosemary asked as she waited for Ian to close the door.

"Nobody. Just a friend from across the hall," he told her, wondering why he suddenly felt lower than a snake's belly. He looked at Rosemary, his hot date. Blond hair, legs that went on forever, some pretty impressive cleavage showing above the neckline of her little black dress.

He wondered how soon he could get rid of her.

FRIDAY NIGHT, Madeline met April McCallum and Annabelle Reardon at the Austin Eats diner next door to Maitland Maternity, racing in about twenty minutes late.

She slid into the booth alongside Annabelle, smiled at April, who sat across the narrow table. "Thanks for agreeing to meet here instead of at the mall. I'm so sorry for the last-minute change of plans. Mrs. Halstead kept saying, 'Just one more question, please.' But I think she's okay now. Poor thing, she spends all her free time on the Internet, looking up ways to scare herself."

April sipped soda through a straw, then sighed. "I know how she feels. I mean, I didn't have to worry about all the problems of a multiple pregnancy, but the problems that can arise *afterward* certainly aren't minimal. I can scare myself silly about the babies, and I'm a trained neonatal nurse."

"It's *because* you're a trained neonatal nurse that you can scare yourself so badly," Madeline said reasonably. "You just know too much, have seen too much. Besides, those babies are fine."

April smiled weakly. "I don't know, guys. I should be doing handsprings, but I just...well, I just worry, that's all. I love those little scraps so much. So much," she repeated, blinking back tears.

"Yes, you do love them, April," Annabelle, the baby of this trio of women, said with a wink at Madeline. "Along with a certain new husband you're pretty gaga over, right?"

"Oh, and look who's talking," April countered, nudging Madeline in the ribs. "Have you seen the way our little girl here looks at Zachary Beaumont, our esteemed obstetrician? Some of those looks could melt rock at fifty paces."

"That's not true!" the young delivery room nurse protested, blushing. "I have nothing but the greatest respect for Dr. Beaumont."

"Oh, yeah, here we go. She *respects* him. Let me count the ways. She respects his yummy chocolate brown eyes. She respects that sexy smile. And, oh boy, does she *respect* the way that man looks in scrubs. Did I miss anything?" April asked, leaning her elbows on the table, which only goaded Annabelle into more protests.

As April and Annabelle went back and forth, Madeline pretended to read the menu she already knew by heart, as Austin Eats wasn't just convenient; the food was good, so good that the place had become almost a home away from home for the Maitland Maternity staff.

Madeline felt comfortable here, comfortable with these two women she both liked and admired.

She'd watched April closely these last months, ever since the birth of the quadruplets last December. What a conglomeration of complications that had caused! The birth mother, hardly more than a child herself, had disappeared shortly after the birth of the quads, leaving behind a note that she wanted April to care for her babies. April, who had been assigned to the quads at birth, had fallen completely in love with them.

The desperate teenage mother had seen that, even the local child welfare agency had seen that, but April's application to become foster mother to the babies once they were able to leave the hospital had been tabled, and all because she would be a single mother.

April had been devastated, and everyone at Maitland Maternity rallied around her, did everything they could to help change the agency's mind.

Madeline had written a long letter to the child welfare board, detailing April's exemplary work ethic as a neonatal nurse and assuring them that medically, as well as emotionally, April would be a perfect foster mother for those abandoned children with their special needs.

And they were special needs babies; premature, needing constant care, requiring close monitoring until at least their fifth year of life, as not all problems showed up immediately after birth. She sometimes felt that she had to educate the whole world about multiple births, and she never backed down from a fight.

Madeline ran a finger down the list of specials as she remembered the day Adam's brother, Caleb McCallum, had entered the picture. A whirlwind courtship and marriage followed, but those first weeks of marriage had been pretty rocky for her friend. And yet, as Annabelle said, April was definitely gaga over Caleb now, and the man couldn't be more obvious about being in love with his wife.

It had become a ritual for Madeline to stop by the nursery every night before she went home, to watch April and Caleb with their babies, the babies they'd both come to love. And now they were a family, at least a foster family, and if the courts had any brains at all, they'd be a real, permanent family.

Because Jenny, the quads' mother, had at last been located and seemed to still want April to care for her children. If she would give her final legal approval to the adoption, all of April's and Caleb's worries would be over.

"Okay. Let's order, eat and get this girl to the mall. It's makeover time," April said.

Madeline immediately felt her stomach clench. "Oh, do we have to?"

April's expression as she looked at Madeline said, *You're kidding, right?*

"Oh, no, Madeline, we have to do this," Annabelle, younger and less tactful, blurted. "You *have* to do this. I mean—look at you."

Madeline looked at her comfortable cotton granny dress. Slightly scooped neck, cap sleeves, button front, a little bit of smocking over the bosom, high waistline. Pretty little blue flowers on a gray background. Short gray cotton vest sweater hanging over the dress. Okay, so maybe the sweater was a *little* baggy. "What? What's wrong with this?"

"Annabelle?" April said, covering her smile with one hand. "You want to take this one?"

Annabelle's cheeks turned rosy, and she stammered slightly as she said, "Oh! Oh, Madeline, I…I didn't mean. I mean…I don't want to *criticize.…*"

"Oh, sure you do," April said cheerfully. "Start with her sandals, why don't you?"

"My sandals? What's wrong with them? I thought you were talking about my clothes, not my sandals." Madeline sat back, sighed. "Oh, all right, all right. It's not like this is the first time I'm hearing this. Ian keeps telling me I must shop in the dark. But the thing is, I *like* my clothes. They're comfortable."

"So's going around naked, Madeline," April countered, "but I don't think it'll ever catch on."

Their food arrived, double cheeseburgers all around, but Madeline had lost her appetite. "How do I explain this?" she asked, addressing the French fry in her hand. "Okay, here goes. I was an only child. Neither Mom or Dad had the faintest idea how to raise this daughter they'd ended up with due to one of those fabled menopausal pregnancies. They never really adjusted to me, so I had to adjust to them. Which meant I spent most of my time with my nose in a book and not thinking about the latest fashion fads."

"That still doesn't explain why, at nearly thirty-five, you're dressing like a throwback to the sixties. Or did you grow up in a commune?"

Madeline lowered her head. "Just until I was twelve," she admitted, then looked at her friends, who were goggling at her. "No, seriously, I did grow up in a commune. It was wonderful. Really. Stop laughing."

"I can't help it, Madeline," April said, wiping her eyes. "I'm trying to be serious, but I keep seeing you tripping through a meadow, a daisy chain in your hair, a loaf of homemade bread under your arm."

Annabelle clapped her hands for attention. "Another discussion for another time, ladies. Okay, so now we know where the granny gowns and sandals and that braid came from—and may they all leave quickly, please. But we're here together tonight to turn Madeline Sheppard from—and I mean this in the nicest way, Madeline—dull and dreary and into *ka-wow!*"

"Oh, sure." Madeline groused, wiping her hands on her paper napkin. "I can see it now. I open a couple of buttons on this dress, take off my reading glasses—which means I won't be able to see my French fries—take down my braid, shake my hair free and—bam!—suddenly I'm Catherine Zeta-Jones.'' She rolled her eyes. ''Cut me a break.''

''Hey, it could happen.'' April ignored the sarcasm. ''And another thing. Are you saying that there's something under that dress that would be improved by opening a couple of those buttons? I'll bet you are. Well, then, we're on our way, aren't we, Annabelle? Hot dog!''

''Oh, no,'' Madeline moaned, and buried her head in her hands.

Chapter Two

Madeline walked to the tall T-stand and lifted off a hanger, holding up the soft cotton flowered ankle-length dress to her friends. "See? It's not just my mother sending me her efforts, sewn with her two arthritic hands, bless her. There have to be dozens of these dresses here. How can you say I'm out of date?"

Annabelle and April exchanged pained meaningful glances. "I'll take this one," April volunteered after a moment. She relieved Madeline of the dress, which she then shoved onto the rack. "Madeline. Sweetheart. Honey. Yes, they still make these dresses. Yes, they still sell these dresses. *To teenagers.* You're thirty-five years old."

"Thirty-four," Madeline grumbled under her breath. "Maybe for only one more day, but I'm hanging on with both hands, thank you anyway."

"Thirty-four, thirty-five, whatever," April continued, taking Madeline by the elbow and steering her toward another section of the largest department store in the mall. "The point I'm trying to make is that, if you're not either eighteen or pregnant, the time has come to say goodbye to the cutesy, little-girl look, okay?"

Madeline cast one last look over her shoulder at the

rack of dresses, sighed. "Okay, but what do I tell my mother? She sends me at least ten new dresses a year."

"Tell her you still want them to donate to the thrift shop run by the hospital auxiliary. Those high waistlines, those gathered skirts? Your mom puts enough material in those dresses to take a woman carrying sextuplets into her third trimester. In fact, maybe you ought to think about donating your entire wardrobe to the hospital thrift shop."

Madeline blinked back sudden tears. "You sound just like Ian. I swear, if that man had his way, all women would wear nothing but bikinis."

"Really? He's a sexist?" Annabelle asked.

"No, not really. I was exaggerating," Madeline said. "He just thinks it's time I paid more attention to myself, that's all, instead of taking the easy way out, which is what he calls my clothes. Which are *comfortable,* not to belabor the point. I don't even have to waste time like this—shopping. You have both figured out that I *hate* shopping, right?"

"Ian said you should pay more attention to yourself?" April nodded, pulling out a soft pink silk blouse, holding up the hanger. "Sounds like a smart man. Life in a commune, working your way through college and med school, working twelve-hour days at the new unit? I know you're busy, Madeline, but you're not just a doctor. You're a fun, lovely, intelligent woman. It's about time you stopped hiding behind those yards of material."

There was no getting around, over or under these two women. She'd have to tell the awful truth. "I've got a gut," Madeline said quietly, so quietly that Annabelle leaned closer, made her repeat what she'd said.

"A gut," Madeline said, more loudly than she'd intended. "A belly, Annabelle. I always have. There are the medical terms for it, but in layman's terms, I'm an apple. You know—apples and pears. Pears have small waists, flat bellies, bigger hips, heavier thighs. We apples have skinny arms and legs, narrow hips, but tend to gain all our weight in our bellies, waistlines. And our busts,'' she added, knowing that every drawback had at least one bonus, and her generous bust was hers.

"She says she's an apple," Annabelle said to April, shrugging.

April shrugged in return. "So? I'm a pear. I've been waging war on my upper thighs since I was twelve. No problem. We camouflage.''

Madeline rolled her eyes. "Isn't that what I've *been* doing?''

"Madeline,'' April said reasonably, "you could hide *Oklahoma* under that dress. We don't need that much camouflage. We just go for short skirts—to show off your legs—and longer, more swingy tops, to hide this massive waistline you say you have. Now, what size are you?''

Madeline tried to make her one-hundred-and-forty-pound, five-foot-six-inch frame smaller—knowing she couldn't make it disappear. "I don't know. I have to go larger to be able to comfortably button my waistbands, which is just another reason Mom's dresses are easier and definitely more comfortable. And slacks? Forget it! By the time the waist fits, the crotch is at my knees, the seat sags, and my legs disappear. Which—'' she ended on a sigh ''—is why I don't wear slacks or jeans.''

"Oh, have *you* ever been shopping in the wrong stores. Except you don't shop, right?'' Annabelle shook her head. "Come on, Madeline, it's just us girls here. The size?''

Madeline sighed. "A fourteen? A sixteen?''

"Sixteen? No way!'' Annabelle exclaimed, eyeing Madeline with what looked to be a practiced eye. "You probably just chose the wrong designers. Some seem to design for those of us with smaller waists and bigger butts—pardon my French—and others design for, what did you call yourself? Oh, yeah, an apple. We just have to find a designer who caters to apples."

"And elastic waistbands," April added, dragging Madeline across the carpeted floor to yet another section of the women's department. "According to my mother, a definite apple, elastic waistbands are the greatest invention since sliced bread, or something like that. A sixteen? Never! I'll bet you're a twelve, once we find those elastic waistbands."

April was wrong. Twenty minutes later, with Annabelle running back and forth between dressing room and selling floor to exchange sizes, Madeline stood staring at herself—and wearing a size ten.

The collarless Wedgwood blue silk suit jacket she wore had long sleeves, a lovely row of covered buttons, a hem that hit just at the top of her thighs and a softly nipped-in waist that actually gave her a shape. A real shape. And the skirt? Lined with slinky taffeta, the straight skirt—with elastic waist—barely skimmed the top of her knees, exposing her slim, well-shaped, very long lower legs.

"Now I ask you, ladies and gentlemen, who *is* this gorgeous creature?" April asked, obviously quite pleased with herself. "So, Madeline? What do you think?"

"I think I don't believe it," she answered, pulling up the tag hanging from the sleeve. "A *ten?*"

"Welcome to the wonderful world of camouflage," Annabelle said as she hung up rejects, then sat on the small chair in the dressing room. "You look great, Madeline. Professional, yet sexy. We'll take it, right, April?"

"Definitely. Happy birthday, Madeline," April answered with a grin. "Thank heaven the mall is open late for the pre-Easter sales. Now that we know the style and the size—and the great elastic secret—Madeline, it's time to pull out the plastic, because we aren't leaving here until you've got a whole new wardrobe. Suits for work, slacks and tops for casual wear, you name it."

"And then we do the shoes, the purses—because you're *not* going to ruin that suit by carrying around that knitted feed bag anymore, Madeline."

"And makeup," April added, unwrapping the elastic tie around Madeline's braid, unwinding the braid itself. "Oh, would you look at those curls! Madeline, you've been hiding naturally black, naturally curly hair? How could you? That's positively criminal. And you've got fabulous skin, Madeline, white and creamy. That's probably because you've never worn makeup. Snow White skin, Snow White hair—all we need now is a prince."

"Yes, definitely a prince," Annabelle said, jumping up from her chair to kiss Madeline's cheek. "You look *wonderful*, Madeline."

"True, Annabelle, but there does come a time when we all need a little…embellishment. Even princesses. With those brown eyes, I'd say some two-tone beige and brown shadow, some peachy-colored blusher and lipstick. And, of course, mascara and eyeliner. Madeline? Madeline, are we pushing too hard? Are you okay with this?"

Madeline, who had been staring at her reflection, half frightened, half pleased, knowing she still wouldn't give Catherine Zeta-Jones a run for her money—but, then, who could?—just nodded. "Okay. Sure. I mean—" she gave her head a small shake, watched her curls settle onto her shoulders "—sure. Let's do it."

IAN LOOKED at his watch, calculating how much time it would take to get across town to the Lone Star in time for their six o'clock reservations.

He'd had it all planned so carefully. Up early, go for a run. Golf with the guys, a nap, some power shopping to locate a reasonably good birthday gift, dinner at six.

Except he'd come home to a note Madeline had slipped under his door, telling him that she might be a little late because she had to go back to the mall with April and Annabelle for "some last-minute idiocy."

Ian pondered that line for a while, then tossed the note aside, found the channel changer and surfed for whatever sports might be on the tube the week before the NCAA March Madness started next week. He lucked out with a great game for one of the last divisional tournaments and settled in to watch, one ear listening for Madeline's footsteps in the hallway.

Not that he wasn't interested in the game on the screen, because he was. But he and Maddie usually watched the games together. Baseball, basketball, football, ice hockey—anything that wasn't soccer, because she always fell asleep during soccer games.

Maybe, after dinner, they'd come back and watch the video he'd rented last night. He'd started to watch it by himself, but only five minutes into it he knew Maddie would love it, so he'd ejected the tape. Then he'd read two chapters of a book. Then he'd walked around his apartment, straightening up, and found one of Maddie's hair clips under the kitchen table. He put it in the dish on the counter, the Maddie Collection Plate that she raided every time she ran out of hair clips or needed postage stamps, emery boards, even her extra pair of reading glasses. Her sandals he kept in the hall closet, along with a tweed vest he hoped she never remembered she owned and the crutches she'd used that summer she broke her foot.

Not that he minded that Maddie, left to her own devices, could quickly have his entire apartment littered with her stuff, because he didn't. He liked that they were so comfortable with each other that they just about lived in each other's pockets. Sharing, caring. All that good stuff.

Except now Maddie was going to turn thirty-five. If he'd thought she'd panicked at thirty, it had been nothing to compare with the teary monologue he'd listened to one night a few weeks ago, wherein Maddie lamented her single state, her ticking biological clock and her conviction that she was speeding headlong into old maidhood.

He was also going to be thirty-five. Did that mean he was racing down the road to old bachelorhood?

Not according to Maddie, Ian remembered, as he looked into the mirror above his dresser, twisting his tie into a neat Windsor knot.

"You're just entering your prime," she'd told him—accused him, actually. "Men have it so much easier. You'll be able to take your pick of women—especially younger women—well into your fifties. But not women. And especially not if we want babies. Do you know how much more difficult it is to even *become* pregnant for the first time after the age of thirty-five? And the complications of having your first child after forty? Not good, Ian, not good. Trust me. So I'm thinking about getting pregnant. I mean, why not? Women like me are doing it every day. Of course, I'd have to find a donor."

"Yeah?" he'd said, trying to keep the conversation light. "Well, don't go to strangers."

Ian checked the collar of his shirt, still looking at his reflection as he thought over Maddie's words, his flip reply, the rather shattered look that had passed over her features before she'd smiled, laughed rather hollowly.

Was that when everything had changed?

Probably.

Maddie was his best pal, his good buddy—his other half, when he got right down to it. There was nothing they didn't know about each other, nothing they couldn't share—not their pains, their joys, their highs, their lows. Theirs was the friendship of a lifetime, the sort only a few were blessed to have and one he knew had to be fed, nurtured, in order to endure.

Except he'd been taking advantage of Maddie. Oh, not intentionally, but he'd been monopolizing her time all these years while keeping his social life in full swing.

Was that his fault? If Maddie didn't date very often, didn't actively look for dates—was that his fault?

Did he keep her that busy? Sure, they saw each other every day, sometimes sharing breakfast in her apartment, sometimes meeting near the hospital for lunch. Madeline cooked dinner for them at least four nights a week.

And on Friday and Saturday nights Ian went out on dates…and Maddie stayed home to read medical journals.

"You've been getting all the perks here, bucko," Ian told himself as he ran a comb through his dark hair. "You don't just count on Maddie hanging around, waiting for you to show up in her life—you *expect* her to be there. And that's not fair."

Maddie should be married. Ian knew that. She should have a gang of kids, definitely. But if she stayed with him, let him be the platonic man in her life, she'd never find a romantic man for her life. Maybe Maddie didn't see that, but he did. Now. The damn dirty shame was that he hadn't seen it for fifteen long years.

"Yeah, but don't tell her that tonight," he warned himself as he went to the closet and pulled out his sport jacket, slid his arms into it as he headed out of the bedroom. "Happy birthday, Maddie. Go away, find a life." He shook his head. "Oh, yeah, that would do it. That one would nail down that Prince of the Year award for sure."

But what else was he to do? What Maddie wanted, what Maddie needed, he couldn't give her. They were friends, not lovers. Hadn't they tried that back in college? It hadn't worked then and it wouldn't work now. They knew each other too well to change their comfortable friendship into something so much more complicated.

Besides, if he tried to kiss her, tried to do anything at all, she'd probably laugh at him, just the way she'd done the one time he had tried to kiss her in something other than a brotherly way.

What was it she'd said to him at the time? Oh, yeah. Something really nice. "What, are you nuts, Russell? I'm not even blond."

"See?" Ian said to the ceramic dalmatian Maddie had bought him for Christmas, the one that stood sentinel in front of his gas fireplace in the living room. "That's how she sees me, Spot. Playboy of the western world. Not that I haven't done my best to live up to that reputation. But man, Spot, I'm getting tired. Dancing all night, ruining my new sneakers with romantic walks in the rain, fielding veiled questions about how many kids I'd like to have. Who needs the hassle? I'm just getting too old for this. Right, Spot?"

Spot just sat there, that sort of sickly half smile on his face that had gotten him marked down to half price and won the heart of Maddie, who believed the underdog should be able to catch a break from time to time. So she'd brought Spot home, given him to Ian, saying he shouldn't worry, she'd feed the mutt if he'd walk him.

Ian smiled, shook his head again. What an idiotic present. He wouldn't take Spot's weight in diamonds for that stupid, crooked-mouth dog.

Okay. He checked his watch one more time, decided he'd killed enough time on introspection, or whatever in hell it was he'd been doing—and he certainly wasn't going to examine his rambling thoughts too closely, because then he might find out. Maddie should have been knocking on his door fifteen minutes ago, maybe twenty.

"Yeah, well, if the mountain won't come to Muhammad," he grumbled, scooping his car keys from the table beside the couch. "Don't wait up," he called over his shoulder to Spot, and headed across the hall to Maddie's apartment.

"GO AWAY!"

Ian knocked again, harder this time.

Madeline should have known. The man never had taken direction well.

There was that time she'd told him not to make a U-turn at that intersection with the No U-Turn sign. Yes, she'd been called to the hospital for an emergency, and yes, she'd wanted to get there as fast as possible. But did he listen? No. That one had cost him a hefty fine.

And then there was the time—okay, about six hundred times—she'd told him not to take the wooden spoon from a pot, take a taste and put the spoon back in the pot. And then he'd wink at her, the rat.

Or the day he swore he wasn't too sick to go camping with some old college friends and ended up with pneumonia. That had been a big "I told you so" between them, considering she had been the lucky one who'd ended up playing nurse for a very uncooperative patient.

She could go on. And on. The man was a menace.

There were times she threatened him with divorce—and they weren't even married.

"Ian, go away!" she called, definitely in the grip of panic. "I'm...I'm not ready yet."

"Well, I am, Maddie. Come on, I'm starving," he called through the door, then turned the knob—just as Maddie realized she hadn't locked the door. Damn him for knowing she rarely remembered to lock the door during the day. He'd give her another lecture. Just what she didn't need, someone else telling her what was best for her.

Madeline turned on her heels, ready to make a break for it all the way to her bedroom, to her bathroom, to the door that would lock behind her once she was in the bathroom.

"Whoa!"

Too late. Madeline remained where she was, her back to Ian, her eyes closed as she waited for whatever would follow that whoa.

It wasn't long in coming.

"Maddie? Is that you? In *slacks?*"

She looked at herself. At the tangerine-colored silk top that flowed softly over her body, ending at the tops of her thighs. At the beige raw silk slacks that were pencil thin all the way down to the ankles, where they covered her brand-new beige boots with the three-inch heels.

She raised a hand to grab the tortoiseshell pendant that hung to her waist from a thick gold chain and turned to confront Ian. "Don't say a word," she warned him.

And, for once in his life, the man was obedient, because he stood there, looking at her. And looking at her. And looking at her.

"Oh, for crying out loud, Ian!" she complained when she couldn't stand it anymore. "*Say* something."

He shook his head, spread his arms. "I can't. I don't know what to say." He used the sweep of one hand to encompass her hair, her face, her new clothing. "What happened?"

Madeline threw up her hands. "I knew it. I just knew that would be your reaction! I look ridiculous. Stay here, I'm going to go wash my face."

His hand snaked out, capturing her elbow. "Oh, no, you're not. Come here, Maddie," he said, half dragging her toward the mirror hanging over a table beside the front door. "Look at yourself. Your hair looks great, all pulled away from your face and curly and everything. And those eyes! Maddie, when did your eyes get so big?"

"Makeup," she told him tightly. "My eyes didn't grow, Ian. It's just makeup."

"I know that, Maddie," Ian said, giving her a quick hug as she faced the mirror. "And I love this color," he said, rubbing a bit of the fabric of her shirt between his fingers. "Silk. I'm crazy about silk."

Madeline shivered, knowing it wasn't cold in the apartment, and stepped away from the mirror, wrapping her arms around herself. "Then you don't think I look ridiculous? It's why we went back to the mall today, Annabelle and I. To have my hair and makeup done."

And then her shoulders slumped. "Oh, Ian, I can't believe I let people *do* this to me. Makeup, a new hairstyle, enough new clothing that I doubt my charge card will cool down for at least a year."

"You mean there's more?" Ian said, waggling his eyebrows at her. "You bought more than just this one outfit?"

"Oh, stop grinning," Madeline said testily. "And, yes, it's true. All your fondest dreams realized. I promised to get rid of my old wardrobe. Are you happy now?"

"Hey, I'm not brokenhearted," Ian said, shrugging. "You look good, Maddie, damn good. Except I never realized you're so skinny."

Madeline's mouth dropped open, and she blinked several times. "Skinny? You think I'm *skinny?*"

"Well, maybe not skinny-skinny, if you know what I mean. I just didn't realize you had any shape at all." He winced, obviously knowing he'd stuck his foot in it, badly. "That is, I know you've got legs. Great legs, Maddie, honest. It's just the rest of you that I didn't know was there. No! That's not right. I *know* you're here, Maddie. I've always known you're *here.* You're my girl, right? You've always been my girl. I just didn't realize you're also *a* girl. No! I don't mean that, either. Oh, dammit, Maddie, let's go eat, okay?"

"Sounds like a plan," Madeline said, grabbing her new purse—much smaller than a feed bag. "It's either that, or we stay here while you make a jerk of yourself. Come on, I'm starving."

Ian spread his arms, looking sheepish and silly at the same time. "Isn't that what I've been saying?"

Madeline rolled her eyes and headed for the door, hiding her smile. *Skinny.* Ian thought she was skinny. Did life get any better than this? Happy birthday, indeed!

IAN HAD ALWAYS gotten a big kick out of watching Maddie eat.

He'd learned long ago that Maddie compartmentalized her life. At work, neat and organized. In the kitchen, wildly creative and definitely sloppy. Meticulous about her checkbook, her drinking-glasses cabinet, her spice rack...while sometimes he teased her that the housekeeping police were going to come get her if she didn't stop using her floors and furniture as her personal clothes hamper.

So neat and orderly in some ways, so "oh, who cares?" in others.

Maddie's food fell into the "Who cares? I do!" category, definitely. It could take her, conservatively, five minutes to explain to the waiter exactly how she wanted her steak cooked, how well-done the onion rings should be, how crisp the spinach salad, how browned the garlic bread. And she'd watch, closely, to make sure the waiter wrote it all down. Ian had long ago learned to tip, heavily, if he planned on ever bringing Maddie back to the same restaurant and actually not have to watch the entire wait staff turn in their aprons and run for the doors.

Then she ate. Heartily. But it was a bite of meat, followed by a bite of potato, followed by a bite of salad. She saved her food, a bit of everything, making sure she got a taste of everything, and all the food got gone at the same time, all while she tsk-tsked at him because he ate his salad first, his potato second and his meat last—and had the nerve to call *him* compulsive.

Ian, having finished his steak, sat with his chin propped on his hand, his elbow on the table, and watched as Maddie enjoyed the remainder of her meal. Bite of salad. Bite of potato, scraping the inner skin to get all the best bits. Bite of steak. "Good to the last bite?" he asked, grinning at her.

"Delicious," she agreed, then glared at him. "You're watching me again, aren't you? Why do you do that?"

"Because it never ceases to amaze me that you don't, for instance, run out of potato before you run out of steak. How do you do that?"

"Planning," Maddie told him. "You should try it. Besides, I'm just naturally a very orderly person."

Ian sat back in his chair. "Sure, you are. Oh, by the way? If you're looking for your Rolling Stones CD, it's under my couch cushion, where you left it."

"It is?" Maddie leaned forward, her eyes wide—and still beautifully huge. He knew the makeup had something to do with this new look, but he didn't care. She was still Maddie—she was just, finally, living up to her potential as a woman. "I looked all over for that yesterday. What if I sat down? I could have broken it. Why did you leave it under the cushion?"

He shrugged. "Because you're such a neat and orderly person? I figured you put it there on purpose. Just like I left your gold signet ring on the bathroom sink. Because you're neat and orderly and probably want it there."

"But I wanted to wear that tonight, Ian. I looked all over for that, too." She closed her mouth, tipped her head as she looked at him. "Are we arguing?" she asked, narrowing those chocolate brown eyes of hers. "Are you trying to tell me I'm taking over your apartment with my *stuff* again?"

"I like your stuff," Ian answered, more honestly than he'd intended. "I like seeing it lying around. I may be crazy, but I'll probably miss it all if it ever goes away."

"Oh," Maddie said quietly. "That's…that's nice, Ian. Thank you."

"You're welcome," Ian said, trying to smile. Except he didn't really feel like smiling.

He knew why, too, which was really upsetting.

He wasn't smiling because Maddie had all but told him during that monologue of hers a few weeks ago that she was going husband hunting. That new hairdo, the makeup, the definitely interesting V-neck tangerine blouse and sexy slacks—they all subtly screamed, "Here I am, Bubba, come get me!"

He couldn't blame her. She wanted a husband, a home, a family of her own. At thirty-five, it was time, maybe more than time.

But what about *him,* dammit? What was he supposed to do without her? What *would* he do without her?

Could he do without her?

Ian protectively caught himself against the edge of the table as a sudden, hearty slap on his back sent his upper body forward.

"Ian, you devil, you! I haven't seen you in a while. How's it going?"

Using the arms of the chair to boost himself to his previous position on the seat, Ian turned his head, looked, then stood up, held out his hand. "Blake. Good to see you. I thought you were out of town this week."

"I was, I was, but I was able to take an early flight back from Phoenix this morning. I was going to call you later, so this is lucky. Are we still set for that meeting next Wednesday? You've definitely talked my board into taking you guys on for the Lattimer project. You're quite the salesman, Ian, although you might want to think about catching up on your social skills. For instance, who is this lovely lady? Aren't you going to introduce us?"

"Oh, sorry," Ian said. "Maddie, I'd like to introduce a business associate of mine, Blake Ritter. Blake, Dr. Madeline Sheppard."

"Doctor? No," Blake said, bending over the hand Maddie extended to him, making a total ass out of himself—in Ian's opinion—by kissing it. "You couldn't be a doctor. You're not old enough to be a doctor. Ian, it isn't like you to rob cradles."

"Down, boy," Ian grumbled, taking his seat. "Maddie is most definitely a doctor—a fertility specialist, as a matter of fact—and most definitely all grown up."

Blake was still looking at Maddie, still smiling at Maddie. "She most certainly is. Well, please don't let me interrupt your date."

"Oh, it's not a date," Maddie said, and Ian fought the sudden impulse to kick her under the table, warn her to shut up. "Ian is just treating me to a birthday dinner. We're old friends."

Blake—handsome in a blond, surfer-boy-cowboy kind of way—looked at Ian. "Old friends? Ian, buddy, have you considered getting glasses?" Then he turned to Maddie while reaching in his pocket, pulling out his business card, employing a gold pen to scribble something on the back. "Dr. Sheppard? I'm having an open house at my new place tomorrow afternoon and would be honored if you could join the party. Two to five, and the two of us could go to dinner afterward—to help celebrate your birthday. I've written the address on the back of my card. Ian? You're coming, aren't you?"

"I can't," Ian said through clenched teeth. "I'm in a two-day golf tournament, and my tee time tomorrow isn't until eleven. Sorry."

"I'm not," Blake said, carefully placing his business card in Maddie's hand, gently closing her fingers around it. "Old friends, huh?" he said. "Ian, I think you're losing your touch."

Ian watched Blake, his custom-made suit and lizard cowboy boots snake their way through the tables to join a willowy blonde at a small table in the corner. Bubba, called up as if by magic, to hit on his Maddie. Damn.

Then he looked at Maddie, who had popped the last piece of steak into her mouth as if nothing was wrong. "You're not going, right?"

"I'm not? Why not? Isn't he a business associate? He

seems very nice. And quite handsome. I even have an outfit in mind.''

"He's...he's a *lech*," Ian heard himself saying, just like some Victorian father warning his daughter away from the local Lothario.

"A lech. Oh, right." Maddie rolled her eyes. "Come on, Ian, he's just a man. And that was the point of all this, wasn't it?" she asked, indicating her new hairdo, her new clothes. "April and Annabelle will be *so* pleased. It's just what they wanted to have happen."

"Bully for April and Annabelle," Ian muttered under his breath. "Come on, we'll have dessert at home."

"At home? Ian," Maddie said, her face lighting with pleasure, "did you buy me a birthday cake?"

"Something like that," he said, calling the waiter over so he could pay the bill. "Well, actually, no, I didn't. But you're inventive, Maddie. I bet you'll figure out a way to put a birthday candle in a bowl of popcorn."

"We're staying home and popping popcorn?" Maddie asked, and her eyes were dull, clouded. "I thought—oh, never mind. Sure, let's go home."

Ian felt like a rat, which was happening entirely too often, and had yet to be the least bit comfortable. "You wanted to go somewhere else?" he asked. Where would he take her? He never *took* Maddie anywhere. They just went places together. Now, if she was his *date,* he'd know what to do. He'd take her dancing. Definitely dancing.

"Maddie?" he asked as they walked to his car. "How about we go dancing? After all, it is Saturday night, and it is your birthday."

She stopped beneath one of the overhead lights in the parking lot, looked at him. "Dancing? Ian, we've never gone dancing. In fact, the only time we've ever danced together was three years ago, when we took those western line-dancing lessons at the YMCA.''

He shrugged, grinned. ''There's a first time for everything, Maddie. What do you say?''

She looked at him, her eyes shining, and nodded. And Ian began to wonder just what he'd gotten himself into this time…and if it was a good thing or a bad thing.

Chapter Three

Madeline dragged Ian by the hand as she made her way through the crowd around the dance floor and flopped in her chair, a hand pressed to her chest, trying to catch her breath.

"No more, no more," she protested, laughing, gulping air. "When do the geriatric line dances start?" she asked as Ian raised a hand, signaling for the waitress to bring them another round. "Oh, good. Yes. Definitely another drink. I think I'm dehydrating."

Ian took a white linen square from his back pocket, leaned across the small round table and pretended to pat perspiration from Madeline's forehead. "You were great, Maddie. I forgot the steps halfway through, did you notice? I turned left, then right, and backed myself straight off the dance floor. But some very nice lady in a Dale Evans outfit—with Day-Glo pink plastic fringe—helped me catch up on the steps."

"Where is she?" Madeline asked, half rising in her chair to look out over the crowd still on the dance floor. "Oh, okay, I see her. Wow, she's good!" She smiled at the waitress and took the glass of white wine from her, downing half of it in one thirsty gulp.

"Whoa, birthday girl," Ian warned her, taking the glass

from her hand, placing it on his side of the table. "That's your third, if we count the glass you had at dinner. You know two's your limit."

"*One's* my limit, Ian," she corrected, trying not to giggle. "When I have two, my whole face starts to tingle. But, hey, this is a special occasion, right? A girl only turns thirty-five once." She rubbed the palm of her hand over the tip of her nose. "Good thing, too. Who'd want to turn thirty-five *twice?*"

"Lots of women, probably," Ian told her. "In fact, if you want to, you can turn thirty-five again next year, and for the next fifty years. I'll never tell. That's what friends are for, right?"

Madeline plopped her chin on her hand as she smiled at him. "Definitely. And you're such a good friend, Ian. I don't know what I'd do without you."

"Yeah, well you don't have to find out," he answered, and Madeline frowned, because he suddenly sounded so serious.

"Ian? Is something wrong?"

"Wrong? Why would anything be wrong?"

"Because you've got that little *thing* going with the nerve in your left cheek," Madeline said reasonably. "Feel it? There it goes again. The last time you did that was the day your garbage disposal did its Vesuvius act twenty minutes before the dinner party we threw for your folks' fiftieth anniversary. Remember? Salad fixings *dripping* from the ceiling."

She watched as Ian put a hand to his cheek, covered the slight tic. "There are times, Maddie," he complained, "I think you know me entirely too well."

"Sorry," she said, then giggled. "Oh, Ian, now my teeth are going numb. You'd better not let me near the rest of that wine." She leaned closer. "Tell me about Blake Ritter. He's handsome enough. Is he nice?"

"Nice? Blake? Sure, he's nice. If you like guys who evict widows and orphans for a living."

"Oh? He's a banker? That's probably very good. Being a banker, I mean."

Ian shook his head. "Maddie, are you listening to me? Hell, are you listening to *you?* I know you're on this husband-hunting kick, but show some discretion, okay? Or don't you know what Blake will think if you show up at his open house tomorrow, bells on, to let him take you to dinner?"

"No, I don't know what he'd think," Madeline said, blinking at him. Was it warm in here? She was definitely feeling very warm. "What would he'd think?"

"He'd *think,* Maddie, that you were willing," Ian told her with a sharp nod of his head.

"Willing?" Madeline blinked, wondering why she'd never noticed how handsome Ian looked in the semidark. His features a little hawkish, very cleanly cut. And with his eyelids narrowed and his expression so *intense,* he looked positively sexy. Even slightly dangerous. Or maybe it was the wine? "Willing to do what, Ian?"

"Oh, for crying out loud." Ian exploded, getting up from his chair and holding out a hand to her. "Come on, Maddie, let's dance."

Madeline began to put her hand out to him, then hesitated. "But...but this is a slow song."

"Your point?" Ian countered, grabbing hold of her hand and pulling her to her feet. "Come on, I think we can muddle through."

"But...but I don't slow dance, Ian, you know that. I'll be all over your toes."

"What else is new," he said, winking at her as he

stepped onto the dance floor, stopped, turned and drew her into his arms. He took her right hand in his left, curled both their arms in, pressed against his chest, so that Madeline had no choice but to raise her left arm, settle it on his shoulder, tip her head so that the top of her head sort of snuggled against the side of his chin.

He smelled of the aftershave she'd bought him for Christmas, the one she'd sniffed at the department store and decided was just what the sexy man-about-town should smell like as he went out on hot dates.

His hand was warm as he held hers. Warm, and dry, and big enough to make hers feel small. He was big enough to make her feel small. And protected. And safe.

And something else.

Uncomfortable.

"Oops, sorry," Madeline said as she stepped hard on his instep. "But I did warn you."

He pulled her closer, laughed quietly, called her his favorite drunk.

Was that it? Was she drunk? She didn't think so. She'd had a single glass of wine at dinner, and that had been hours ago. She'd sipped the second glass here at the club, and Ian had taken the third glass away from her. She couldn't be drunk.

Okay, so what was she? Why was she feeling sort of…sort of *tingly?* And *aware.* Aware of Ian. His hand on the small of her back. His warm breath tickling her ear. His long legs lightly bumping against hers. His strong chest, so delightful to lean against. His hips, so…no, she wouldn't think about his hips. Or her hips. Or how close his hips and her hips were as they danced.

What was wrong with her? This was Ian, for pity's sake. She hadn't felt this way about Ian in forever! Not since she'd figured out that he was the love-'em-and-leave-'em type, and if she wanted him to stay around, then they had to be friends, not lovers.

So she'd tamped down any other feelings, physical feelings, she had for him, and had concentrated on being his friend. And they were great friends. The best.

For fifteen years, she had depended on him, and he had depended on her. She'd watched his girlfriends come and go, and come and go, and come and go, but he had never left her. They were connected, that's what they were. Connected by friendship, and friendship was almost as good as love.

Wasn't it?

The song ended, and suddenly Madeline realized she was standing in the middle of the dance floor, *draped* all over her best friend. Dancing only looked logical as long as the music kept playing. Once it stopped, you were just two separate people, hugging each other in public.

Madeline pulled her hand free, smiled at Ian. "Well, that was fun," she said, her cheeks feeling stiff, her tongue slightly thick. "Can we go home now?"

MADDIE WAS QUIET all the way home, sort of sunk into the leather bucket seat, her chin on her chest. In fact, Ian thought for a moment that she'd fallen asleep, but then she sighed—a deep, rather heartfelt sigh—so he knew she was still awake.

He turned on the radio, pushed the buttons until he found the basketball game and tried to concentrate on the play-by-play. But it didn't work. All he could think about was Maddie, sitting next to him so silently. Maddie, smiling at him, stars in her eyes. Maddie, filling his arms as they swayed back and forth on the dance floor.

Maddie. His good friend.

Maddie. A woman he no longer recognized. No more

the safe, sensible Maddie who always wore rubbers when it rained and checked the expiration date on the milk carton every time she took it from the refrigerator shelf. No more the Maddie who schlepped around in shorts, an oversize sweatshirt and a pair of pink bunny slippers definitely past their prime. No more the Maddie who wore those shapeless, ankle-length dresses that went well with the tight braid she wore—and nothing else.

This new Maddie even stood up straighter, dammit.

And when had she learned to flirt? Because that's what she'd been doing with Blake Ritter. Flirting. Oh, sure, she'd sounded so innocent when she'd told him, "We're just good friends," or whatever drivel she'd said while batting her big brown eyes at the guy who'd just kissed her hand.

Kissed her hand? Ian flexed his hands on the steering wheel, once more feeling the itch on his palms he'd felt when Blake had put on his Sir Galahad act.

We'll go to dinner. Fat chance. *We'll go to bed.* That's what Blake had meant. He knew that. Didn't Madeline know that?

And then a small voice spoke from behind a recently opened door in Ian's brain. *And just what business is it of yours anyway, bucko? You don't own her.*

I don't? Ian silently asked that small voice. *Then why do I feel like I do?*

Do the words "selfish bastard" ring any bells? the little voice asked, dripping sarcasm. *No? Well, how about these? You can't have your cake and eat it, too. How about those words? Then, as long as we're at it, how about dog in the manger? That means you don't want her, but you don't want anyone else to have her, either. Which, when you get right down to it, is pretty much a synonym for selfish bastard. Am I getting through here, sport?*

"Ian? You missed the turn," Madeline said from the passenger seat. "Ian? Do you hear me?"

"Thanks, Maddie," he answered, grateful that her voice had finally drowned out that little voice, the one he was pretty sure had to be his guilty conscience. "I, um, I thought we'd take the scenic route."

"Ha! You missed the turn, Einstein. Admit it."

"Did not, Miss Manners Politeness School dropout," he countered, happy that Maddie once more seemed to be in a teasing mood.

"Did so, which-way-did-he-go doofus," she said...and they were off, laughing and joking with each other as he drove around the block, headed into the apartment complex.

Madeline had just topped his "Miss Just-shot-the-ball-into-the-wrong-basket" with "Mister Do-you-mean-toothpaste-tubes-have-*tops?*" as Ian inserted the key in his front door, then stood back so she could enter first.

Madeline immediately sat down on the edge of the coffee table and bent over to unzip her short boots, kick them off. "Oh, God, I've wanted to do that for the past three hours. I *hate* high heels."

"And there goes the glamour," Ian teased as she stuck out her legs and wiggled her toes. He picked up the boots and set them side by side under the coffee table. "But, please, Cinderella, now that you're home from the ball, can you wait a little longer to get back into your customary rags? I kinda like the view."

Madeline got up, padded over to the minibar in her stocking feet. "Don't worry, I won't be going back to my customary rags, as you so sweetly put it. I've got a whole new casual wardrobe. It'll knock your socks clean off, buster."

Ian grinned as she disappeared behind the bar, resurfaced with two bottles of soda. "What? No more wine?"

"Please," she countered, rolling her eyes. "I'm just beginning to be able to feel my lips again." Then she frowned, looked at the soda bottles, left them on the bar. "Coffee. I'll make coffee. *Black* coffee."

Ian followed her into the kitchen, watching as she measured grounds into a filter, then started the coffeemaker. "You're not drunk, you know," he told her as he observed her quick, efficient movements. "You've just had a good time tonight, that's all."

"And I can't recognize the difference?" she asked, looking at him owlishly. "Now that's depressing. How long has it been since I've had a good time?"

"How long? Well, let's see. You busted your butt for way too many years of college, med school, your internship and residency. You worked day and night for about the last year, getting all your ducks in a row for the new multiple birth wing. Now that it's finally up and running, you're working days, nights, weekends. I don't know, Maddie—how long has it been since you've just…let it all hang out?"

"I may have been twelve," Madeline said, pulling a face. "That is depressing, isn't it?"

"Definitely," he said, opening the cabinet door, reaching in to grab two coffee mugs. He turned around, the mugs in his hands, and realized that he was standing directly in front of her. "But you had fun tonight?"

She tilted her head, smiled at him. "Oh, yes, Ian. Definitely."

Her smile had a very strange effect on him. It squeezed his heart until it hurt.

"Coffee's ready," Madeline said as she looked at him, as he looked at her. "Ian? Coffee's ready."

"Huh? Oh, okay," he said, giving his head a quick shake. What was the matter with him? There had to be something the matter with him, because he'd been about to kiss Maddie. He'd really been about to kiss her. And none of that good-pals-kissing-on-the-cheek stuff, either. A real kiss.

Maddie took the mugs, filled them, then spooned sugar into both of them, one teaspoonful for her, two for him, just the way he liked it. "Here you go," she said, handing him the mug then walking past him into the living room, oblivious to the fact that she'd almost gotten thoroughly kissed.

She sat down on the couch, her long legs propped on the coffee table, as usual. She held the mug with both hands as she carefully sipped the hot coffee, watching him over the rim. "Ian? What's wrong? You seem sort of on edge. Is this about Blake Ritter? Because if it is, don't worry. I won't accept his dinner invitation."

"But you are going to the open house?"

"Are you kidding? Did you see the address he wrote on the back of that card? The guy has got to have built himself a *mansion*. Of course I'm going. How often do I get to see a mansion?"

Ian walked to the bar, set down his mug, picked up the soda bottles in preparation of returning them to the small refrigerator. "Have aspirations of grandeur, do you?" he asked. "Madeline's mansion. Okay, I admit it. It does have a certain ring to it."

"Yes, it does, doesn't it? But, no, I don't think so. Who raises children in a mansion? And I'll bet the local mansion-owners' organization frowns on swing sets in the backyard and bicycles in the driveway. Although I do want a house someday, definitely. My balcony just isn't large enough to grow all the herbs I want, and there's nothing like homegrown vegetables and fruits. No preservatives, no pesticides. We only ate organically grown food in the commune, you know. You've never really tasted broccoli until you've tasted homegrown.''

"I've never really tasted broccoli, remember," Ian said, faking a horrified shiver. "All green and lumpy. I can't even look at it too long. Hey," he said, trying to change the subject before Maddie began one of her lectures on the rip-roaring benefits of beta-carotene, "don't you want to open your present?"

Madeline's head came up, and she sniffed like a hound gone on point. "Present? Present? I have a present? I thought dinner was my present.''

"Dinner? For the big thirty-fifth? Oh, I don't think so," Ian teased as Madeline put her mug on the table, slid her feet to the floor, stood up, approached him with narrowed eyelids.

"Where is it?" she asked him, as there was no obvious big box with a ribbon and bow on it anywhere in the living room. "Come on, Russell, talk to me. Where's my present?"

"Oh, no. It's not going to be that easy. Remember the rules?"

"Ian, you wouldn't! I want my present. I don't want to—oh, all right." She grabbed his hand and led him over to the couch, told him to sit down. She sat beside him, one leg crossed beneath her, and leaned toward him. Maddie and her new perfume and her big eyes and her—yes, dammit, her cleavage—leaned toward him. She took a deep breath—and there was that cleavage again—let it out slowly and asked, "Animal, vegetable or mineral?"

Ian waggled his eyebrows. "Mineral."

"No! Mineral? Really?" Maddie wriggled a little on the couch in her excitement. Probably because she hated him, liked to see him suffer. Worse, she was oblivious to the fact that he was suffering. Just looking at her, having her so close to him, was putting him through the tortures of the damned. But she couldn't know that. How could she know that? Up until tonight, he hadn't known it.

"Second question," he prompted her.

"Well, I'm not going to ask if it's bigger than a bread box. Not since you said it's mineral. Unless you bought me a hunk of lava, or moon rocks, or something."

"Damn, why didn't I think of that?" Ian said, slapping a hand to his forehead.

"Very funny." Maddie tipped her head to one side, obviously cudgeling her brain to come up with the best question she could ask.

"Okay," she said after a few moments, moments during which Ian wondered if there were any monasteries near Austin, because he probably should go find one, put himself behind locked doors before he just gave up, grabbed Maddie and kissed her senseless. "Second question. Put it on a table or wear it?"

Ian grinned. "We're talking about you, right?" he asked her.

"Yes, we're talking about me."

"Okay, then the answer is both. Because everything you wear eventually ends up on a table, or a sink, or— and this happens a lot—a floor."

"Ha, ha, very funny," Madeline retorted, her forehead wrinkling as she went back to concentrating on formulating what would be her final question.

Ian was caught between this completely unexpected animal attraction and thinking about how the so brilliant, so professional Dr. Sheppard could sometimes resemble nothing so much as a little girl on Christmas morning.

"Come on, Maddie," he pushed. "There is a time limit, you know."

She waved her hands in front of her, saying, "I know, I know, don't rush me. Okay, I've got it," she said then, sitting back slightly, grabbing her bent knee. "Question three. Planned, or just because you had to have one?"

"Huh?"

She rolled her eyes. "I said, planned, or just because you had to have one. Tell me, Ian. My present—did you buy it just for me or just so you had something to give me?"

Were the walls starting to close in on him? Certainly the room was getting smaller, shrunken down to little more than the space needed for one couch and two bodies—one excited…and the other *excited*. And probably about to blow this one, big time.

Ian played for time. "The rule, Dr. Sheppard, is an either-or question. Simple, direct, to the point—or points, since I get to choose between two. Your question comes under the final exam for Psych one-oh-one, and it's an essay question, no doubt about it."

"No, it's not, Ian. It's either-or, just like in the rules. And besides, it's my birthday. So answer the question. Please?"

He felt one side of his mouth drawing up into a crooked smile. What the hell. He might as well go for it. Wasn't honesty always supposed to be the best policy, or something like that? "I bought it for you, Maddie," he said. "Just for you, just because I wanted to, okay?"

"Okay," she said quietly, then sat back, folded her hands in her lap. "No more questions, not that I've been able to guess."

"Then I can give you the present now? You're sure? And remember, no shaking of the box, turning of the box upside-down, rattling of the box. None. Or have we forgotten the oil lantern I bought you two years ago? Remember? The one I so helpfully put oil in before giving it to you? I still can't get the stain out of the carpet.''

"I can't spill *mineral*, Ian," she said, slightly miffed. "Now come on, I want to see my present."

Ian reached behind him, into the space between the arm of the couch and the cushion, and drew out a fairly flat, oblong box wrapped in red foil, topped with a gold ribbon bow. He still didn't believe he'd gone into the jewelry store, let alone bought Maddie's present there. Not when he'd been certain he was going to buy her a telescope for her balcony.

"Here you go, Maddie. Mineral, smaller than a bread box, bound to be found on the kitchen counter within a week. Happy birthday, honey."

Madeline looked at him. Looked at the box. Looked at him. Looked at the box.

"Take it," Ian told her, laughing. "It doesn't bite, honest."

She took it, held it gingerly, as if maybe he was wrong, and it could bite. "Jewelry? You bought me *jewelry?* Oh, Ian, I—"

"Don't thank me yet, Maddie, you might not like it."

"Not like it? Ian, how could I not like it? You bought me *jewelry.* Last year you bought me a food processor. Oh, not that I don't *love* it, because I do—but *jewelry?* I think I'm going to cry."

"Rule six hundred and twelve, Maddie," he told her. "No crying."

Madeline blinked rapidly. "I don't think I can promise that, Ian. Not after the last few days I've had. I barely know who I am anymore."

Ian frowned, confused. "You, too? That is—what do you mean, Maddie? Your clothes?"

"My clothes, yes. My clothes, my hair, the lipstick I'm wearing. Strangers asking me to dinner. Going dancing. You giving me jewelry. I'm probably going to wake up any minute now, but not before I open this present."

With that, she popped off the stick-on bow, then ran a fingernail beneath the tape holding the paper on the box. Slowly, while Ian fought the urge to grab the box from her, offer her a really cool telescope in exchange, Madeline removed the paper until she was holding the slim velvet-covered box in front of her with both hands.

"Here goes," she said, drawing in her breath, opening the box. "Oh! Oh...oh, *Ian!*" She touched the bracelet with one hand, stroking its length, not taking it out of the box. "Oh, Ian, I...I...oh, Ian!"

"They call them tennis bracelets, for reasons the salesman couldn't give me," he said, clearing his throat halfway through the explanation, because something was stuck there, constricting his airway. "He also said all women like diamonds. You do like diamonds, don't you, Maddie?"

He'd been speaking to her bowed head, as she kept stroking the length of diamonds set in gold. And then she lifted her head, looked at him, her huge brown eyes bright with tears. "I can't believe this. Your birthday's in two weeks. How am I going to top this, Ian? Do you even want your own yacht?"

He relaxed, just a little. Smiled, just a little. "So you like it?"

"I *love* it," she told him as he took the box from her, freed the bracelet from the small elastic bands that held it in place. She put out her right arm, and he slipped the bracelet around her wrist, fastened the clasp. Lifted her hand to his lips, kissed it.

Hey, anything Blake Ritter did, he could do—and better.

"Thank you, Ian," Madeline said, using the tip of her left index finger to stroke the diamonds, watching as the bracelet slipped round and round her wrist. "I'm never going to take it off. Never."

And then she leaned forward, laid her hands on his shoulders and kissed him square on the mouth.

Not that she meant it to be anything more than a friendly kiss. A thank-you kiss. A kiss between friends.

Right?

And who cared? It was a kiss. It was on the mouth. Her hands were on his shoulders.

And his brain went on Stun.

Ian slid his arms around Madeline's back as he drew her closer so that she was kneeling on the cushions, then falling forward, sprawling on top of him as he angled backward until his head was on one arm of the couch.

He pulled back slightly, angled his head as he caught her mouth once more, caught it as she opened her lips, probably to tell him to let her go. He couldn't let her tell him to let her go.

With the tip of his tongue, he traced her lips, skimmed over her teeth...plunged into her mouth. He moved his arms so that his hands gripped her on either side of her waist, tensed as she moved so that she now lay completely on top of him, her right leg slipping between his thighs.

She had to feel him, be aware of how aroused he was, how much this definitely was *not* a kiss between friends, old pals. Buddies.

He let his hands find the hem of her blouse, that softest silk blouse that could be burlap once compared with Maddie's silken skin. His fingertips burned as he stroked her sides, skimmed his hands higher, found his way across her back to the hooks holding her bra shut.

With a dexterity born of long practice—not that he wanted Maddie thinking about that right now—he opened the hooks. One, two, three. He moved his hands again, wishing he didn't feel so nervous, like a sixteen-year-old in the back seat of his dad's Oldsmobile.

His right hand closed over Maddie's breast, and he swallowed the sigh she breathed into him.

Could this be happening? He and Maddie, together? He and Maddie, about to make love? After all these years…

"What the hell?" Ian tensed, feeling the tingle against his stomach.

Maddie pushed herself away from him, straddling him as she sat up, reached under her blouse, pulled out the vibrating pager she'd clipped to her waistband.

"A pager? You took your *pager* along tonight? You told me you weren't on call. Dammit, Maddie, you're not on duty every last damn minute, you know."

But she wasn't listening. She was already disentangling herself, those long legs leaving him so that he lay there, feeling angry, frustrated, confused…and not a little stupid.

"It's the hospital," she told him, heading for the phone, punching in numbers. The perfect professional, just as if she hadn't been lying on top of him fifteen seconds ago, being groped, giving every indication that she was enjoying being groped.

Ian sat up, took in several deep breaths, then stood, went to the minibar to pick up his mug of lukewarm coffee. He watched Maddie as she talked, listened, talked some more, all while holding the phone between ear and shoulder, her left hand abstractedly spinning the diamond bracelet.

"I've got to go," she said as she put down the phone, reached for her boots. She sat on the edge of the coffee table, struggled into the boots. "Dammit, look at this. Zippers on shoes. I don't need this hassle. It was so much easier with my sandals, but these slacks are too long, so I have to wear the heels. I could have been out of the door by now, if I had my sandals."

Ian smiled. He couldn't help himself. This was the Maddie he knew, the Maddie he loved. The most down-to-earth, unaffected, *honest* woman he'd ever known. "There's trouble with one of your patients?"

She nodded as she stood up, stamped her feet a few times, quickly downed the remainder of her coffee. "Maggie McCallum. She's spotting, and frightened out of her mind. I'm not officially on call, and I won't treat, since I did have that wine. Zachary Beaumont is already there, but I've got to go. She asked for me."

"Then you go if you have to, but I'll drive if you do," Ian said, not that he believed Maddie would stay if he'd asked her to stay. They could talk later, tomorrow. Talk about what happened tonight. If either of them could figure out what had happened tonight. But, right now, and for as long as it took to deal with Maggie McCallum, Maddie's entire mind would be concentrated on her job, doing her job.

"Oh, you don't have to—thank you, Ian. I'd appreciate it."

Maddie picked up her purse, headed for the door. "Maddie?" he called after her as he grabbed his car keys from the table.

"Huh?" she asked, one hand on the doorknob.

"I don't want to be overly picky, but—"

"What, Ian? We have to go."

"Yes, I know. But I was thinking—first you might want to rehook your bra."

"Oh, *damn!*" she said, her cheeks flushing as she dropped her purse, reached her hands behind her, under her blouse. "Oh, stop smiling. It isn't funny!" Then she quickly opened the door as Ian followed after her, laughing out loud.

Chapter Four

Madeline tapped her fingertips on her thighs, an outward sign of her inner wish that Ian's car had wings and they could be across town now, at the unit.

She knew Maggie McCallum, knew her to be a steady, levelheaded woman. An intelligent woman. But she also knew that all the intelligence and maturity in the world meant less than nothing to an expectant mom who'd started bleeding two months into her already at-risk pregnancy.

Maggie would hold on, give an outward appearance of calm. But inside? Inside, she'd shake, cry, silently scream against the unfairness of it all.

Madeline's job would be to get through to Maggie, and to Adam, as well. While Zachary took care of his patient medically, it would be Madeline who had to calm the expectant parents, keep them operating as part of the team, not another problem for the team.

"Maddie?"

"Hmm?" Madeline said, mentally rehearsing what she'd say, how she'd handle a small problem…how she'd deal with a much larger one.

"How bad is this for the McCallums?" Ian asked,

neatly maneuvering his car through a yellow caution light before it could turn red.

Sighing, Madeline folded her hands in her lap, at last aware that she'd been fidgeting. "There's a lot of schools of thought on it, Ian, and a lot of studies, statistics, that sort of thing."

"How so?"

"You really want to know?"

"Believe it or not, yes, I do. As a matter of fact, I've recently developed this whole new interest in intricacies of women and pregnancy."

"Really," Madeline said, sniffing. "Okay. Spotting in the first trimester isn't that unusual and often goes away on its own. Many believe that bed rest, and enough carefully administered drugs, will handle this sort of complication nine times out of ten. Then there's my nature's-way mother, who says that a pregnant woman can stand on her head for nine months, but if the pregnancy isn't to be, it isn't to be. Those are the two ends of the spectrum, and probably always will be. The main thing, right now, is to reassure Maggie that nothing she did caused the spotting."

"And that would be your job, right?"

"It would," Madeline said, sighing once more. "The job doesn't stop when the couple gets pregnant. We're working as a real team effort in the unit. Once the pregnancy is confirmed, mine becomes the role of cheerleader, confidante, hand-holder, you name it. Oh, I hope she's all right."

"You trust Zachary Beaumont?"

"He's the best," Madeline told him, realizing that Ian was trying to keep her talking, helping her to convince herself that there were high chances for a good outcome for Maggie's quints. "Cool in a crisis, reassuring and one

of the top obstetricians in the country. If anyone can get
Maggie and her babies to a safe delivery, it's Zach.''

"The McCallums can't ask for more than that, can
they? So you and the rest of the team do everything you
can, and then you hope for the best. What else can you
do?''

"Nothing. And worrying won't change that, will it?''
Madeline turned her head, looked at him. "You're right.
We do our best, then hope for the best. Okay, I'm calmer
now, thanks. It's just that, although every set of hopeful
parents are special, Maggie and Adam really have gotten
to me. And not just because Adam's father donated the
new unit. They're special people, that's all. They deserve
a break.'' She put a hand on the buckle of her seat belt.
"Oh, good, we're here.''

Ian pulled right up to the front doors. "I'll let you out
here, go park the car. Do you mind if I come up to the
unit, wait for you?''

Madeline felt a sudden stinging behind her eyes, threat-
ening tears she hadn't expected. She put her hand on Ian's
arm. "I'd really like that, Ian. I'd like that very much.''

He covered her hand with his, gave hers a squeeze.
"Maddie? About earlier tonight. I know that's never happened before, and I—''

She cut off his words with her mouth, a quick kiss that
was all she had time for, when she wanted the rest of their
lives. "I'll see you upstairs," she said, then quickly exited
the car, trotted toward the main doors, not even noticing
that the boots pinched her toes.

Adam McCallum was waiting for her just outside the
elevator doors, his short dark hair spiking on his head, his
hazel eyes clouded with worry. "Doctor! I'm so glad
you're here. Maggie's down there…just down the hall.
Dr. Beaumont is still with her.''

Madeline nodded, and the two of them set off down the hallway together. "Would you please tell me what happened tonight? When did the spotting start? Any cramping? Discomfort of any kind?"

"No, no, nothing like that," Adam told her, stabbing his fingers through his hair. "We had an early dinner at the country club, then came home, popped in a video. Maggie was fine, fine. She just went into the bathroom to get ready for bed, and all of sudden I heard her crying, calling out for me. I brought her right here."

"Which was exactly the right thing to do. She's in good hands."

"Yeah, then tell me, Dr. Sheppard, why am I still so scared?"

"Madeline. I'd be honored if you and Maggie began calling me Madeline. After all, we're going to be seeing a lot of each other over the next seven months."

"Thank you." It had been the right thing to say, and she watched as Adam McCallum's shoulders dropped slightly and his body relaxed. "But are you sure we're going to have the next seven months, Madeline?"

"Nothing's a sure bet, Adam, but Maggie's very healthy, the babies are developing nicely, and this is probably just a small speed bump we have to get over, that's all. Now, if you'll stay out here for a few moments, I'd like to go talk to Dr. Beaumont and Maggie."

Ten minutes later, Madeline was sitting in a chair pulled up beside Maggie's bed, with Adam standing on the other side, holding his wife's hand.

"Speed bump," Adam said, his smile shaky. "Is that the medical term?"

"If not, maybe it should be," Madeline told him, "because that's what this looks like to everyone. There's been no increase in bleeding. In fact, there's been no more spotting since Maggie was admitted to the unit. She isn't cramping or in any pain. Temperature, normal. Blood count back, and good. Blood pressure, normal. And she's hungry. As a matter of fact, if you're this good tomorrow morning, Maggie, Dr. Beaumont is going to kick you out of here."

Maggie McCallum dabbed at her moist eyes with a pile of the ridiculously small tissues all hospitals handed out to their patients. "I was so frightened, Madeline. I've never been so frightened in my life."

"And we're going to avoid that in the future, aren't we?" Madeline said, looking at Maggie with some intensity. "You and Adam are prepared to do anything and everything possible for your children, right?"

"Of course," Adam said, sounding not only confident, but a little angry at being asked the question. "And you said Maggie hadn't done anything wrong."

"No, she didn't. And I'd hoped Maggie could continue her normal routine for a while longer, but tonight's episode tells us that we're going to have to go into full pamper-mommy mode now. And that, Maggie, means that you'll be handing in your resignation at school, effective Monday morning."

"But—but my students. They won't understand. I can't just desert them, just not show up. Can I?" she asked, looking at Adam.

"She can't go in and say goodbye?" Adam asked Madeline.

"Not Monday, no. When Maggie goes home, she goes home to bed rest. No lifting, no driving, no cooking, no vacuuming—that's the worst, you know—and no emotional farewells at the school. In a couple of weeks, once Dr. Beaumont okays it, you can visit your class, Maggie, maybe have a little party, if it's allowed."

Adam bent over his wife, kissed her forehead. "I'll call the principal tomorrow," he said with a reassuring smile. "It'll be all right, sweetheart. And I'll enjoy spoiling you, although I will tell you that it amazes me, the lengths you'll go to get breakfast in bed."

Maggie sniffled, laughed weakly, nodded her agreement. "We said we'd do anything, didn't we, darling? I guess we just hit our first *anything*." Then she turned to Madeline. "Will I be on bed rest for the entire pregnancy?"

"I don't think so, but that's up to Dr. Beaumont. Let's just take this one day at a time, all right? And now, considering that it's nearly one in the morning, I'd say it's time for Maggie to get some rest. You, too, Adam. Go home, get some sleep and be back here around ten tomorrow morning, when Dr. Beaumont makes his Sunday rounds."

"No, that's okay, Madeline," Adam told her. "I've already made arrangements to stay here. Someone is bringing a cot in here for me."

"Oh, yes, just one more service of the McCallum Multiple Birth Wing," Madeline said, smiling. "Just remember, new unit or not, a cot is still just a cot, so don't blame us if you wake up with a sore back. Adam, could I speak to you for just a moment? Outside?"

"Madeline?" Maggie asked, pushing herself up against the pillows. "What are you going to say that I can't hear? I thought you said everything's fine."

Madeline looked from Adam to Maggie, then shrugged. "All right. I was planning to tell you separately, but there really isn't any compelling reason for that, is there? Maggie, you do know how you got into this condition, don't you?" she asked, gesturing toward Maggie McCallum's still fairly flat belly.

"Certainly," she answered, frowning. "Testing, timing, fertility drugs..."

"And?" Madeline prompted.

"Sex," Adam said abruptly. "We made love."

Madeline grinned. "Give that man a cigar, and a cold shower, because sex is something you two are *not* going to be having for a while. Deal?"

Madeline watched as Maggie's cheeks colored prettily, as if she were a young bride. "Adam?" she asked, looking at her husband.

"Maggie?" he said right back at her, then grinned. "So, how would you like me to teach you how to play gin rummy?"

Laughing, Madeline left the expectant parents alone and headed into the hallway. Crisis averted. Maggie and Adam, totally onboard with the team for the duration. Madeline, exhausted. Completely and totally exhausted...until she looked down the hallway and saw Ian leaning against the wall, holding two cups of cafeteria coffee.

She approached him slowly, taking in the way his slacks draped slightly over his brown loafers, the way he had his white shirt sleeves rolled up, the top button open, his tweed sports coat draped over one arm. One lock of his black hair fell forward over his forehead, and his bright blue eyes looked heavy-lidded, sleepy.

She could put him on bread, butter him and have him for an early breakfast.

"You're smiling," he said as she stopped in front of him, and he handed her one of the paper cups. "I'll take that as a good sign?"

"A very good sign," Madeline agreed, prying off the lid and taking a sip of the hot liquid. "Oh, this is good."

"Good? Delirious with fatigue, are you?" Ian teased.

"This coffee, Maddie, tastes like it was run through an oil refinery. Twice."

"I know, but I think I'm used to it," she told him as she pushed the button that would summon the elevator. "Ian? How unprofessional would it look if I took off these boots?"

"You'd have to roll up your slacks, remember," he said as the doors opened and they stepped into the elevator. "How about I carry you to the car?"

"You and whose army? No way, Ian," Madeline retorted. "Carrying my hundred and forty pounds all the way to the parking lot would have to qualify you for some Olympic sport."

"Maddie-carrying. It has a certain ring to it," Ian said, leading her through the foyer, through the main doorway and toward the parking lot. "That's it, keep limping. You'll get there. We'll go home, I'll make you some real coffee and then I'll massage your feet. Does that sound like a plan?"

It would have, about eight hours ago. But a lot had happened tonight, and the idea of lounging on Ian's couch, her legs in his lap, his hands stroking her feet? Ian maybe opening his mouth and wanting to talk about just what *had* happened—or almost happened—on that same couch a little earlier?

"I—I probably should try to get some sleep. I'm off tomorrow, but I'll want to go in, see Maggie one more time if Zach is going to be sending her home. I have some photocopied articles in my office on multiples pregnancies that she might want to read."

"So no coffee? No Russell special foot rub?"

Madeline bowed her head. "Not tonight, Ian. But thank you. Really. Thank you." She touched the diamond bracelet. "For everything."

"For everything? Don't mention it. I mean it. Please, don't mention it."

The car moved through the dark, nearly deserted streets, passing beneath street lamps so that Madeline, when she dared to look at him, could see the tic working in Ian's cheek.

This wasn't going to work. They either had to talk about tonight, or she'd have to never talk to him again. It was definitely an either-or situation, a really important either-or situation.

"Ian?"

He braked at a red light, turned to look at her. "Maddie," he responded tightly.

"What...what happened tonight. I guess, that is, I *know* we have to talk about it."

He tapped his fingers against the steering wheel. "Gee, that sounds about as welcome as having a root canal. Was it that bad?"

"No. No! It was wonder—that is, oh, Ian, would you look at us? This is ridiculous. We can't even talk to each other. When have we not been able to talk about anything?"

The light turned green, and Ian concentrated once more on his driving. "Never," he said after a few moments. "We've never *not* been able to talk to each other. About anything. Okay? Does that answer your question?"

"It would have, up until tonight," Madeline told him, keeping her head front even as she kept watching him out of the corner of her eye. "And, if we're ever going to be able to talk to each other again, I think we have to talk about this."

"No, we don't."

"Don't, Ian, or *won't*? Which is it?"

Ian sighed as he turned into the apartment complex,

eased into his assigned parking space. He turned off the ignition, pulled out the key and looked at Madeline. "Nothing's changed, Maddie. We're still friends. I just kissed you, that's all."

"Oh, really? Kissed me? Excuse me, but I think I remember having to rehook my bra."

"Okay, that, too," he said as they both got out of the car, headed toward their building. "We had a moment, Maddie. Your birthday, the wine, that outfit—your eyes. I don't know. It was a moment. Can't we let it go at that? Do we have to psychoanalyze it?"

"Yes," Madeline said as he held open the door for her and she entered the building ahead of him. "I think we do have to psychoanalyze it. And you know why? Because we're friends, Ian. We've been friends for fifteen years, and I don't want to lose that."

I don't want to lose it because your friendship is all I've got of you, all I could ever hope to have of you, and I figured that out years ago. That's what she would have said, if she hadn't quickly bitten her bottom lip until she got a firmer grip on her emotions.

She dug in her purse for her apartment key as they headed down the hallway, but Ian grabbed her elbow, steered her toward his door. "Okay, *now* we talk. How in hell are you figuring that one kiss—yes, and one small grope—are going to cost us our friendship?"

Good question, and Madeline mulled it as, still holding onto her elbow, he opened his apartment door and just about pulled her inside. He probably deserved an answer.

"Sit," he ordered, then gave her a lopsided grin. "Please sit."

Madeline sat, remembering how she'd been sort of *sprawled* on this same couch a few hours ago, sending out silent "Go for it!" signals in response to every move Ian made.

She hopped up from the couch, headed for the kitchen. "There's bound to be some coffee left," she said, hoping there wasn't, because then she could make more, hide in the kitchen, delay the inevitable just a little bit longer.

Ian followed her, not giving her any time, any space, any wiggle room at all. He helped her take down two clean mugs, gathered spoons and sugar bowl. Then he carried the mugs into the living room, set them down on the coffee table in front of the couch. Or the COUCH. Madeline was beginning to think of that particular piece of furniture in capital letters.

But she sat down anyway, because obviously Ian wasn't going to let her go without drinking her coffee or having their talk. She held the mug with both hands, hoping the mug wouldn't shake, spill on her delicate raw silk slacks before the credit card bill even arrived in the mail.

"Okay, cards on the table," Ian began, putting down his half-empty mug. "Here's how I see it. We've turned a corner in our relationship, reached a new level—something. I haven't figured out exactly what yet, but there's definitely been a change. What bothers me is that I'm not that shallow, dammit. I didn't jump your bones because of that outfit, or the eyes, or the hair. I mean, I didn't just look at you tonight, say *wow*, look at her, why not—and then go on the attack. As a matter of fact, now that I think about it, you kissed *me* first."

"Oh, brother! Well, there it is, isn't it? I knew we'd get to it. It's *my* fault? Is that what you're saying, Ian? That it's *my* fault? After all, it's my outfit, my eyes—my *hair*. And you're right, I did kiss you first. Shame on me! Well, let me go get frumpy again, so you don't lose control of your libido, okay?"

"Maddie," Ian said, his voice low, his expression pained. "I'd really appreciate it if you listened to *everything* that I said. I admit it, you really threw me a curve tonight. I'd be an idiot not to admit that. But what I'm trying to say to you is that I saw this coming. I've seen it now for a couple of weeks. Why do you think you're wearing that bracelet instead of a telescope?"

"People can't *wear* telescopes." Madeline shot the words back, knowing she was being deliberately dense. She stood up, began pacing in front of the coffee table. "A couple of weeks? Why?"

Ian laid his head back against the cushions, closed his eyes. "You don't remember? You don't remember crying all over me, telling me about your biological clock, about sperm donors, the whole nine yards?"

Madeline stopped pacing, felt the blood drain out of her face. "You volunteered," she said, remembering. "But not nicely, as I recall it. What was it you said? Oh, yeah—don't go to strangers. My God, Ian, is that what you were planning to be tonight? My sperm donor?"

He shot off the couch as if one of the cushion springs had broken. "No! Dammit, Maddie, why are we having so much trouble saying what's on our minds? On my mind, anyway," he ended more quietly, avoiding her eyes.

"I'm sorry, Ian," Madeline said apologetically, trying to regulate her breathing. "Just tell me what you mean. I'll try to understand."

"Thank you. Now, if I knew what I mean, we'd be in pretty good shape," he told her, his smile just about breaking her heart. "Let me reiterate—I did not plan to be your sperm donor tonight. The only reason I mentioned that conversation was to help pinpoint the moment I started thinking about you...differently. As if you were a woman."

"I've *always* been a woman, Ian," Madeline said, blinking back tears. "You mean you hadn't noticed?"

He put both hands to his head, stabbed his fingers into his hair—and ended by looking a lot like Adam McCallum had earlier, nervous, on edge, even frightened.

"The only way this could go any more badly would be if a clown popped up from behind the bar over there, holding a quacking duck in his hands," he said miserably, and Madeline smiled in spite of herself.

"A duck? Why would the clown have a duck with him?"

Ian grinned. "Because all the chickens are busy laying eggs?"

Madeline laughed, feeling some of the tension ease out of the room. Maybe this was going to be all right. Maybe they could still be friends.

Of course, then Ian blew it....

"Here goes, Maddie," he said, sobering. "I mentioned what happened a couple of weeks ago because I've been feeling like a selfish bastard ever since that conversation. Fifteen years, Maddie. For fifteen years, we've been best friends, or I thought we were. But we weren't. And you want to know why? I figured it out. You were my best friend, but I wasn't yours. I kept up my own life, my other friends—women. But not you. If it wasn't school, it was your internship, your residency and now the McCallum wing. You had time for two things, your work and me. Other than that, you had no life. Hell, your mother still makes your clothes because you can't seem to even find time to go shopping. And you can't do that because, when you're not working, you're cooking for me, doing my wash for me, hanging out with me. And then, with this birthday coming up, you finally realized that you're watching your whole life go by without really living it. No man in your life, no kids. And it's my fault.''

Madeline had stood very still while Ian spoke, mentally watching him dig a hole into the carpet, just so she could throw him into it, cover him over with beige plush.

As he spoke, her temper built, then divided, doubled and built again.

''Are you through?'' she asked when he stopped, looked at her like a puppy who needed a reassuring pat on the head. He was lucky she didn't take a two-by-four to him!

''No, there's more. I was sort of slowly working my way to the grand finale. What I'm trying to say to you, Maddie, is that I'm looking at you differently now, and I've realized that I—''

''I don't believe this,'' she interrupted, starting slow, knowing she would be building on block after block of hurt and outrage. ''Do you know how *stupid* you've just made me sound? Poor little Maddie, working and slaving, then coming home and working and slaving some more. I *cook* for you, Ian, because you'd starve otherwise, or your cholesterol would be through the roof thanks to your taste in food groups. Besides, I *like* to cook, and I like to watch you eat. I *wash* for you because my unit doesn't have a washer and dryer and yours does, so it's only fair that I do your wash while I'm doing my own.''

''Maddie, I—''

''Oh, no, don't interrupt me, Ian, because you started this, and now I'm going to finish it. You're right, at least about one thing. I have been too busy to have much of a life outside of my work. I knew that going in—you don't get to be a doctor, a specialist, just by wishing for it to happen. So I wouldn't have had much of a *life*, as you call it, even if you weren't in it. If I chose to spend my free hours with you, with my *friend,* where's the crime in that?''

"Well, I—''

"I'll tell you where the crime is, you stupid…stupid *idiot.* The crime is that I knew what I was doing. From the beginning, I've known what I was doing. Do you think I was never attracted to you? In *that* way?''

"Attracted? Well, I—''

"Shut up! Yes, you idiot, *attracted* to you. For all the good that did me. You were the most popular guy on campus, remember? And you went through willing coeds like Grant through Richmond. Do you really think I wanted to be another notch on your belt?''

"Hey! I wasn't that bad,'' Ian protested.

"Bad enough. Oh, you settled down, grew up, but you still go through women at the rate of two or three a year. Did you really think I wanted to be one of those women? I like you, Ian. I like you, I trust you, I'm comfortable with you—and, yes, I once thought I was in love with you. But you know what would have happened if I'd let you know that?''

Ian opened his mouth, closed it when Madeline glared at him.

"I'll *tell* you what would have happened. I would have been one of Ian Russell's women. Here today, gone tomorrow. I liked you too much to let that happen. So I settled for being your friend, your buddy, your pal. So now, fifteen years later—fifteen years too late—you're telling me you've suddenly started looking at me as more than your friend? You're looking at me as a woman? Well, bully for you, buddy boy, but you're too late. You're too damn late! Now, I've had a long day, a damn long day, and I'm going to bed. Alone!''

And then she made her exit, ruining it only by tripping over her three-inch heels and rolling over one ankle, so that she limped out of the apartment, wrapped in her righteous misery. Catherine Zeta-Jones probably would have been damn proud of her.

Chapter Five

"Yeah, it's a bummer all right. Rain date's next Saturday? Sure, I can make it, partner. Uh-huh, uh-huh. Definitely a rotten break. I'm upset, too. See you, Gregg."

Ian put down the phone and barely resisted doing a joyful dance as he went to the window, looked out at the pouring rain that had turned Sunday morning as gray as his mood had been—until he'd seen that rain. A bummer? A rotten break? He hoped he'd carried off his role of disappointment, considering he was probably headed for golfer's hell, as no golfer is ever happy to see rain.

He turned away from the window, eyed the clock on the mantel. Nine-fifteen. Normally, if he didn't have an early tee time, he'd be in Maddie's apartment right about now, happily downing one of her great breakfasts. Then he'd clean up the kitchen while Maddie showered and dressed—but probably no longer in baggy sweats, which he was already beginning to think he'd miss.

They'd fight over the newspaper—who would get the sports section first—watch the talking heads put their spin on the network shows, yell at the television set a little, sip coffee and nibble on whatever homemade breakfast buns were left over from breakfast.

In the afternoon, they'd go out, visit a gallery, window-shop for stuff they didn't want to buy but liked to look at, grab a meal at one of their favorite restaurants—usually one with a drive-through window.

By the time they'd walked off lunch, maybe caught a movie, the pot roast Maddie had earlier stuck in the oven and put on the timer would be done, and they'd be able to smell the roasting meat, carrots, potatoes, onions as they entered the apartment building.

Dinner, some television, a cutthroat video game or two and then some homemade dessert, a kiss good-night on the cheek, and another Sunday would be over.

Man, he loved Sunday. A guy would have to be seriously crazy not to love Sundays with Maddie.

He patted his stomach as it growled in hunger, and headed for the kitchen, opening cabinets, swearing under his breath, opening the refrigerator door, sniffing the carton of milk inside and swearing some more.

He could have cereal, but without milk. Toast, but without jelly. And orange juice? Forget about it. Maddie squeezed her own oranges, fresh every morning. He hadn't bought a carton of orange juice in fifteen years.

Ian sat at the kitchen table, ran a hand over his mussed hair. And he realized something. It came to him slowly, but he realized something. Something that was probably very important.

He and Maddie sure did eat a lot.

But that wasn't it. That wasn't what he figured out. What he figured out was that food—Maddie's very good food—was a sort of *substitute* for something else. Eating was a sensual pleasure they shared, definitely, but was it also a stand-in for a sensual pleasure they denied each other, had been denying each other for fifteen years?

What *was* he hungry for this morning? Homemade cinnamon buns? Or Maddie? Fluffy scrambled eggs and a slice of ham? Or Maddie?

More important: what would he miss most if Maddie went out of his life? Food? No. Someone to watch sports with on television? No. Someone to nag him to take his vitamins? No. Someone to talk to about his love life? Definitely no, and never again.

He'd miss Maddie. Her smile. Her intensity. Her dedication to her work. The way he felt so comfortable with her, so damn comfortable, like she was the other half of him, the two of them halves of the same whole.

And she'd said, just last night, right here, where he could hear it, that she'd loved him. Once upon a time, Madeline Sheppard had believed herself to be in love with him.

Wasn't that a bitch?

How had he missed it? Where had his head been at the time?

"Probably up my—ah, hell," Ian muttered, and padded toward the front door in his bare feet, wearing a faded gray T-shirt and gym shorts that had seen better days. Maybe he'd just get the paper, hide in basketball stats for a while and try to figure out life—his life, Maddie's life, their life together—some other time.

He opened the door, already bending to grab the heavy Sunday edition—and there was Maddie, one hand raised to knock on his door.

"Maddie?" he asked, looking at her as if he'd never seen her before. This was Sunday morning attire? Slim navy slacks, a fuzzy white angora sweater that went halfway down her thighs? A flowered scarf around her neck, tied low, at her waist? And her hair—once more pulled back off her face, but only some of it, caught up in two combs, with her curls tumbling onto her shoulders. Venus on the half shell had never looked so good.

Damn.

"You're late," she said, then turned on her heels—yup, she was wearing heels again—went into her apartment, leaving the door open behind her.

It wasn't a trail of bread crumbs leading to the gingerbread house, but it was close, and Ian decided not to question, but to follow where Maddie led.

He picked up the newspaper, then smoothed down his wrinkled T-shirt with one hand, tried to flatten his mussed hair and followed his nose, which told him that, yes, homemade cinnamon buns awaited.

He put down the newspaper even as he picked up the tangerine silk blouse, shook his head when he saw the wrinkles in it. Following the trail of bone leather boots, he found the beige slacks draped over the antique telephone stand and the gold chain necklace hanging from the one of the wall sconces Maddie had bought two years ago but had yet to fill with candles.

"I've never looked in your closets, Maddie," he said after dumping everything on her bed and returning to the living room. "Is there anything in them?"

Maddie, who stood behind the bar separating the kitchen from the living room, looked at him, her expression pained. "You don't ever get tired of that joke, do you, Ian?"

"Not as long as you stick around for all the reruns, no," he said, looking at the small table Maddie had set with two places. This was promising. She wasn't going to throw his breakfast at him, she actually planned on the two of them sitting at the same table, sharing their meal.

"Maddie, about last night—"

She held up her hands, including the one with the oven

mitt on it, cutting him off. "There will be no rehashing
of last night. None. Either we move on, try to get back
to where we were, or one of us is going to have to move
to Alaska. You got that? Now come on. I've got to be at
the hospital in a half hour."

"I'll take you?" Ian half offered, half asked.

"Oh, really? And then who does the dishes?" she
asked, carrying a platter piled with fluffy scrambled eggs
and a mound of crisp bacon over to the table. "I think I
can manage getting myself to the hospital, thank you.
Now come on, sit down and eat before everything gets
cold."

Ian sat, but he wasn't hungry. He'd been starving, but
he wasn't anymore. Still, he picked up his glass of fresh-
squeezed orange juice, and the vitamin pill sitting next to
the glass, and availed himself of both. If he didn't, he was
pretty sure there'd be hell to pay, because Maddie, the
best of good sports, could blow higher than the space
shuttle when she finally let loose the reins on her temper.

"How long will you be at the hospital?" he asked as
he scraped some scrambled eggs onto his plate. If she
could pretend the world hadn't exploded last night, so
could he, dammit. At least for another five minutes.

"I don't know. I phoned earlier, and Maggie had a
restful night, or what was left of last night. She feels fine,
there's no more spotting, and Adam has promised to wait
on her hand and foot, and even tie her to their bed, if
necessary, to keep her on bed rest. Zach will probably
release her this morning when he makes his rounds."

"That's good then, isn't it? I'm happy for them, although I wouldn't want to be either of them for the next
few months, until those babies are born."

Maddie chewed on a piece of bacon, then said, "It
doesn't have to be a scary time, an awful time. They'll

be able to enjoy a lot of this pregnancy, if we can just convince them that, in the past few years, multiples are not just more common, but that we've learned a lot about taking mother and babies safely from conception to delivery.''

"But it's still scary," Ian prompted, trying to keep her talking. If he could keep her talking, maybe he'd find a way to tell her what he'd tried to say last night, right before she'd gone into orbit.

"Well, I certainly wouldn't lie and say a multiples pregnancy is as uncomplicated as most single births, no. But multiple births have always fascinated me, you know that. What with both Mom and Dad being twins and everything. Dad's twin died at birth because of complications with the delivery, and he grew up an only child because his mother could no longer become pregnant. I never knew her, but Dad said she mourned until the day she died, and that's so sad. The moment I hit my obstetrics rotation, I couldn't help but zero in on multiples, on infertility, and I immediately knew I'd found my specialty.''

Okay, they were getting closer to the subject. She was talking babies. *Let's talk babies,* Ian thought. "I was wondering, Maddie. Since both your mom and dad were twins, what were the odds that you could have been twins, or could have twins of your own?''

She finished her orange juice, patted her mouth—she was wearing lipstick!—with her napkin. "There have been lots of studies, and there are probability charts, that sort of thing. Still, more often than not, my mother's folklore answer seems to be right on this one, that twins skip a generation.''

Ian coughed, cleared his throat, wondering if Maddie had missed a seed in the orange juice. "Skip…skip a generation? Does that mean you could have twins?''

Madeline shrugged. "Anything's possible, if I were to get pregnant."

Ah, getting closer to the subject. "And you've considered that, Maddie? Having twins, that is. You know, I'd like twins. I think that would be neat."

"Really," Madeline said, and her look, and her tone of voice, told him he'd crossed a line. "Well, I have to go. You'll clean up? I shouldn't be more than an hour, but then I have to think about getting ready for Blake Ritter's open house. Are you going? I mean, obviously your tournament has been canceled?"

Ian's mood, which had been jumping around pretty spryly, zeroed in on righteous anger. "Ritter's? You mean to tell me you're still going? Dammit, Maddie, we have to talk. Not eat, not pretend nothing's happened. *Talk.*"

"Not if I don't want to," Madeline told him. "I said everything I had to say last night."

"Well, *I* didn't!" he yelled, but he was talking to the door that closed behind Maddie as she ran out of the apartment.

MADDIE CRIED all the way to the hospital. She'd cried most of the night, so it wasn't as if this was anything new, but she was getting pretty sick of it.

Why had she thought she could get up this morning, make breakfast, act as if her world still turned on the same axis, moved along with the same routines that had been set in stone for fifteen years?

It had taken everything in her, every scrap of courage, to go across the hall to Ian's apartment this morning, tell him that breakfast was ready. But that's what she had to do if she had any hope of continuing their friendship.

She should have known it wouldn't work.

Not after she'd admitted to him that, yes, she'd once been in love with him.

Why had she said that? For one, it was damning information. And two, there was no *once* about it. She was in love with Ian. Had always been in love with him, would always be in love with him.

Either that, or she was a masochist. Maybe both—because, otherwise, why would she have forced herself to be content with a friendship—albeit the friendship of a lifetime—when what she had always wanted, needed, was his love?

Madeline parked in her assigned spot in the covered garage and walked toward the staff entrance, trying to pick a bit of angora from her tongue as she wondered, not for the first time, why she had bothered to put on another of her new outfits. She liked them, certainly, but who was she kidding? Take away the angora, the scarf, the slacks that really did feel quite good against her legs, and she was still Madeline Sheppard—thirty-five years old, an apple and single. Probably to remain single for the rest of her life.

Because no one could replace Ian in her life, not ever. Even if they could go back to where they'd been, be friends again, be comfortable around each other again. She'd been about as comfortable around him this morning as she'd be standing stark naked, in the dark, in a cactus field. Any way she moved, she felt exposed, and definitely in danger of getting hurt.

Ian probably felt the same way. Poor guy. When she wasn't angry with him, Madeline felt sorry for him. He'd been the victim of April's and Annabelle's makeover, which was probably quite an embarrassment for him. But that was men. They reacted to stimuli and always had.

Although it still shocked her that Ian could lose control just because of a tangerine silk blouse.

Maybe she'd have to think about wearing bright colors more often....

"Good morning, Madeline."

She turned to see Zachary Beaumont coming toward her. "Rounds done so soon, Zach?" she asked. "How's Maggie McCallum? I was just going up to check on her."

The obstetrician shook his head. "Our patient is fine, her babies look great on the ultrasound I ordered this morning, but the husband looks like he needs a long nap. Poor guy, he gets to worry about both his wife and the babies. Maggie is concerned only for the babies and doesn't think about herself at all."

"Isn't that always the way it is?" Madeline said, patting Zach's arm as she leaned forward, hit the button to summon the elevator. "Mothers are always oblivious to their own possibilities for complications. Maybe it's nature's way of keeping them strong and focused on getting those babies safely to that delivery room?"

"Could be," Zach answered as the elevator doors opened. "Well, I'm off. There's a stack of medical journals at home with my name on them, I'm afraid. See you tomorrow?"

Madeline nodded, waved and then stood back as the elevator doors slid closed, opening again on the second floor. She waved hello to the nurses on duty and went directly into Maggie's room, to find her patient sitting on the side of the bed, already dressed to go home.

"Now this is a sight to gladden my heart, even on such a gray and rainy day," Madeline said. "Where's Adam?"

"Oh, he had to go to the office. Something about having our insurance cards photocopied, or something like that." Then Maggie tipped her head, smiled. "You know,

Madeline, it was pretty intense in here last night, but I did notice. I'm noticing again this morning. You look *terrific*."

Madeline couldn't help herself. She smiled, raised a hand to pat at her loose curls. "Thank you. I...I, well, I bought a new wardrobe. It was either that or my friends were going to burn everything I owned and leave me with nothing to wear."

"Really? I'll bet there's a story behind that," Maggie said, then took hold of Madeline's hand as she lowered her arm. "And this! I saw it last night. I mean, who could help it? Diamonds sparkle so beautifully in overhead lights, don't they? Is it new?"

Madeline covered the bracelet with her left hand. "Yes, as a matter of fact it is. A birthday present, actually. I just got it last night."

"Your birthday was yesterday? Oh, Madeline, I'm so sorry. I imagine the hospital was the very last place you wanted to be last night. Especially after that gift. Somebody is very serious about you, Madeline. Can you give me a hint?"

Madeline could feel the blood draining from her cheeks. "Oh, no, no. You've got that wrong, Maggie. The bracelet is from a friend."

"Then he's a very *good* friend," Maggie said, and beckoned to her husband, who'd just walked into the room. "Adam, look at this bracelet. Would you call that a gift from a good friend? Come on, Madeline, stop covering it up and show Adam."

Sighing, Madeline gave in and did as Maggie asked, holding out her arm so Adam could look at the bracelet.

Adam gave a low whistle. "A friend, huh? Madeline, I'm no expert, but I'd say at least one of you has a different definition of the word *friend*."

Madeline felt the color rising into her cheeks. Her entire body seemed to blush. "What…what do you mean?"

"Maybe I can help," Maggie said as Adam hovered over her, helping her to her feet. "Men—and I'm right, I imagine, that the bracelet came from a man?—well, unless they're millionaires, they do *not* give diamond bracelets to good friends. They give them to *girl* friends. *Serious* girlfriends. Getting ready to go down on one knee and propose to her type girlfriends."

As Madeline held out her arm, stared at the bracelet, Maggie asked, "Tell me. This friend? What did he buy you last year, if you knew him last year?"

"Oh, we've been friends for fifteen years," Madeline answered, her ears sort of buzzing, snatches of things Ian had said to her last night coming into her mind, confusing her, beginning to delight her.

"Fifteen years?" Adam chuckled. "Sort of a slow starter, isn't he?"

"Adam, stop it," Maggie told him, playfully slapping at his arm. "Come on, Madeline, tell us. What did he give you for your birthday last year?"

"A food processor," Madeline mumbled into the cowl neckline of her angora sweater, risking another mouthful of angora.

"What? I didn't hear that." Maggie prodded her.

"A food processor, Maggie. She said he gave her a food processor," Adam said helpfully.

"A food processor? And now a diamond bracelet?" Maggie gave Madeline a quick hug. "Oh, I'm so happy for you!"

Madeline vaguely heard Maggie through the buzzing in her ears, over the loud pounding of her heart. "Um…thank you," she said. "But it's not like he's *said* anything yet. He just gave me the bracelet."

"See? I said slow starter, didn't I?" Adam said, earning himself a very stern look from his wife.

"Maybe we interrupted him?" Maggie asked, walking alongside Madeline on their way to the elevators. "Did we interrupt you last night, Madeline? It wasn't quite midnight, so we could have, couldn't we?"

"Hmm?" Madeline knew Maggie had said something, but she hadn't really heard it. She held out her hand to Adam, then to Maggie, mumbled something about seeing the two of them on their next visit to the unit. Then she walked into the elevator, not realizing that the doors closed with both Maggie and Adam still standing in the hallway, watching her, smiling as they watched her.

She had to go home. She really, *really* had to go home, although how she got there would remain a mystery to her for the rest of her life.

"Ian!" she called as she banged on his apartment door, then tried the doorknob and, finding the door unlocked, went inside, slamming the door behind her. She stuck out her tongue, removed yet another bit of angora fuzz, rubbed it between her fingertips. "Ian Russell, where are you?"

He appeared at the mouth of the hallway that led to his bedroom, hopping as he tried to get his second leg into his jeans. "What? Maddie? What's wrong? Is the building on fire? Are you hurt?"

Just look at him. Maddie tried not to smile as he pulled up his jeans, zipped them, sucked in his already flat gut as he closed the button. His chest was bare, which would probably make this easier, and his hair was still damp from the shower. "You had something to say to me?" she asked, walking to the couch, stepping out of her shoes as she went, then sitting down, making herself comfortable.

"What?" Ian came around the couch, stood in front of the coffee table. "*Now* you want to talk? Dammit, Maddie, I used to think I understood you."

"That goes both ways, Ian. I used to think I understood you, too."

"Yeah, well," he said, raking a hand through his hair, obviously searching for words, any words at all. "So did I. But not lately. Lately, I just think maybe I've lost my mind."

"Oh, well, that's flattering," Madeline said, feeling more confident by the moment. She didn't know why and didn't want to examine the why of any of it, but Adam and Maggie McCallum's words had opened her eyes to a whole new world of possibilities.

When she put those possibilities together with a few things Ian had said last night—words about how he hadn't just gone wild because of a tangerine blouse but had already started looking at her in a new way a few weeks ago? And then the bracelet, instead of a food processor or a telescope? And that kiss? The way he'd held her? The way he'd touched her?

Ian pointed at the couch. "May I sit down?"

She nodded, smiled. "It's your couch."

Ian took a single step in the direction of the couch, then hesitated, looked at her. "Do you want a soda? I do. My...my mouth is kind of dry all of a sudden."

Oh, this was fun. This was really *fun*. Was it possible for a person to get drunk on angora fibers? "I'm okay," she said, "but you go ahead. Get a soda if you need it."

"It's not that I *need*—oh, hell, Maddie! What are we doing here? Is this any kind of conversation? I don't think so. I'm sitting down now," he announced, then sat, his bare feet flat on the floor, his hands on his knees, his head facing forward. "There. I'm sitting."

And Madeline was sitting.

They were both sitting.

Sitting silently.

Not moving.

Madeline played with her new bracelet, turning it round and round her wrist.

Ian swallowed hard, coughed into his hand.

The clock on the mantel struck twelve times, announcing the hour.

Madeline waited. She knew this man. She'd known this man forever; he'd been a part of her forever. If she said something now, he'd say something back, and after the way he'd tied his tongue into knots last night, she didn't think having a conversation was the way to go. Better he should give her a quick monologue, without interruptions.

So she'd just wait. Let him say what was on his mind without any prompting. He'd figure out a way.

"I, um, I really didn't explain myself very well last night, Maddie," he said at last, and she kept facing forward, careful not to do anything that would interrupt his flow of words. "And then you interrupted me, wouldn't let me finish...."

Madeline's eyes widened, and she bit her tongue so that she wouldn't respond. Especially since he was right. She had interrupted him. She hadn't let him finish what he had been trying to say.

"Well...not that we're going to rehash that," Ian said, his knuckles white as he squeezed his hands on his kneecaps. "But what I was saying was that I'd been thinking about our relationship—our friendship—the past couple of weeks, and about how I'd feel if you ever weren't a...a part of my life."

Now she did turn, look at him. Not be a part of his

life? How could he think such a thing? "I'd never leave you, Ian. I couldn't."

He sort of nodded, pressed the palm of his hand against his mouth, then slipped his hand around so that he was squeezing the back of his neck. Her heart broke for him. "Oh, God, why is this so difficult? Am I that afraid that you meant what you said last night? That you loved me once, but think of me now as just your good friend? Have I blown it with my lousy timing, Maddie? Please tell me I haven't blown it."

Maddie put her hand on his. "You haven't blown it, Ian. But are you sure? Are *you* really sure?"

He took her hand in his, raised it to his lips. "I love you, Maddie. I'm sure I love you. I'm sure I'm *in love* with you. I don't know how it happened, when it happened, but if you ever left me I don't know what I'd do. I just don't know what I'd do without you."

"Oh, Ian," Madeline said, blinking back tears. "There's a difference between the two of us being a *habit* and being in love. Are you sure?"

"That's the question, isn't it, Maddie? But it's the one I have to ask you. Are *you* sure? I know what you said last night, that you loved me a long time ago. But what about now? Could you still love a man too thick to see what's been right in front of him all these years?"

"I could try," she answered, caught between laughter and tears. "I could certainly try."

She watched as the tic that had been working in Ian's cheek disappeared, as his hunched shoulders relaxed...as that crooked smile crept onto his face.

"Your beeper," he said, holding out a hand, palm up. "Come on, Maddie, you're not on call. Give it over."

She reached under her sweater, unclipped the beeper from her waistband, handed it to him.

He took it, turned it off, set it on the coffee table. "Okay, then," he said, grinning wickedly as he reached for her. "Now...where were we?"

IAN RUBBED a hand towel over his hair as he came out of the bathroom, a large bath towel wrapped around his waist, and looked at the bed.

Maddie still slept soundly, probably a combination of having worked at the hospital until nine last night and then having to put up with an ardent fiancé when she finally got home—not that she complained, the sweetheart.

He'd yet to see any of her new nightgowns or pajamas, although she told him she'd gone back to the mall with Annabelle one day last week and heated up her plastic one more time. But, as far as he knew, her purchases were still in bags dumped on her bedroom floor, and he was getting pretty darn used to seeing Maddie coming toward his bed, dressed in one of his old T-shirts, her long legs bare.

What time was it? He looked at the bedside clock and smiled. He had to meet Gregg at ten, but it was only eight-thirty. Plenty of time.

He walked to the bed, bent low over Maddie and stroked her soft curls from her cheek. "Maddie?" he said softly. "Maddie, I need my T-shirt."

"Hmm?" She moaned, turning onto her back, blinking her eyes several times, trying to focus as she looked at him. "You need your—oh, don't be silly. You can't wear this. I slept in it."

"True, but I need it," he said, suppressing a grin. "I need it on the floor, hanging from the overhead light, thrown over the back of a chair—you name it. I need it anywhere except on you. It's blocking my view."

Maddie raised her arms, stretched like a contented cat. "You know, Ian, if I'd realized what a *thing* you've got about my breasts, we could have gotten where we are a whole lot faster."

"You're just saying that because it's true," he told her as she reached for the towel around his waist. "Hey, who said you could do that?"

"I can't?" she asked, raising her eyebrows. "Then tell me, why am I awake?"

"So I can show you something," Ian said, disengaging her grip from the towel and walking over to grab a magazine from the top of his dresser. "I picked this up yesterday," he said, returning to the bed, sitting down on the edge as he held the magazine cover so that Maddie could see it.

"A *bridal* magazine? You actually stood in line at some checkout counter with a *bridal* magazine? Good Lord, Ian, you *are* in love, aren't you?"

He kissed the tip of her nose. "Was there ever any doubt? Anyway, I was looking through it last night, before you got home, and I found something we definitely have to have."

"Oh, really?" Madeline said, pushing herself up against the pillows. "What is it? His and hers silver shoehorns? Because I'm really sorry I broke your plastic one putting on those stupid boots, but I promised to get you a new one."

"No, not shoehorns," Ian said, paging through the inches-thick book until he found what he was looking for. "Here we go," he said, pulling out a thick card that had been glued to one of the pages, a sample wedding invitation. He handed it to Madeline. "It's not the usual formal invitation, but it's perfect for us. Everything else is up to you, Maddie, I promise, but I think I have to insist on this one.''

She read the outside of the card, then looked at him, tears in her eyes. "Oh, Ian, I love you. I love you *so much!*" she said, then grabbed him, pulled him down on top of her—which was pretty much where he wanted to be anyway.

The card fell to the floor, landing on its back so that the words on the outside were visible: *Today I marry my best friend...*

DELIVERED WITH A KISS
Mindy Neff

Chapter One

Nerves clawed at Annabelle Reardon's insides, but never in a million years would she let it show.

She was the labor and delivery nurse in the McCallum Multiple Birth Wing at Maitland Maternity Clinic, the only specialty clinic of its kind in Texas. At twenty-three she was the youngest person on staff, but she knew her job and considered herself one of the best, a status she strove for in every part of her life.

The smell of antiseptic, pine cleaner and the cafeteria's chicken special permeated the air, scents Annabelle was so used to she hardly noticed.

She held her friend's hand as the orderly wheeled the gurney toward the surgery room. The much anticipated arrival of Maggie McCallum's quintuplets was imminent, and Maggie was understandably scared.

"It's only thirty-six weeks, Annabelle." Maggie panted through the contraction that seized her. "It's too soon."

"Now you stop your worrying, you hear? Breathe through that contraction, sweetie. There's a good girl. We'll get 'em stopped right quick. And thirty-six weeks is perfect—the babies' lungs are fully developed by this time." She squeezed Maggie's hand and didn't make a peep about the bones grinding in her own.

Maggie's father-in-law, Jackson McCallum, had donated this specialty wing in honor of his late wife, who'd died giving birth to triplets, Adam—Maggie's husband—Briana and Caleb McCallum.

But that had been more than thirty years ago. Medical research had advanced light-years since then.

"Zach's kept a close watch on you, Maggie, and you'll be just fine. You know he's the best obstetric perinatologist around."

Just saying his name gave Annabelle a flutter in her stomach. What the devil was wrong with her lately? She'd managed to subdue her attraction for the handsome doctor, but recently the struggle was getting harder—not that he'd given her an ounce of encouragement.

No, her wily hormones were most likely a product of the incessant urging from her stepmother to do some catching up in the dating, man-woman relationship department.

But now was *not* the time to get sidetracked by Dr. Zachary Beaumont.

Regardless of her easy assurances, the procedure ahead of them was filled with potential complications.

Still, Annabelle knew she was darn good at her job. A nurturer by nature, having raised her brother and three sisters, she was cool under fire and knew just the right thing to say to calm a fear or encourage a dream. She believed that everything always worked out for the best in the end.

Idealistic, perhaps, but there it was.

And she intended to see that her friend sailed through this risky delivery with a positive attitude and a minimum of fear.

"I know he's the best," Maggie said, battling tears.

"And I trust you both. Thank you for being here for me, Annabelle."

"I wouldn't be anywhere else. Hang in there, Maggie. It won't be much longer now."

When they got to the doors of the operating room, Annabelle pushed through, then turned.

"Whoa, there." They had an entire entourage following them—the whole McCallum clan, extended family and friends. "This is where the line ends, guys. The waiting room's just down the hall."

Adam McCallum stood firmly by his wife, the stubborn set of his jaw masking sheer terror. They'd gone through a rough time getting pregnant. With his mother's death in childbirth, Annabelle knew that weighed heavily on his mind.

She reached out and put a comforting hand on his arm. "Fathers are the exception. You get gowned up, and we'll let you stand by your wife's head and coach. If you faint, though, I'm putting it on the bulletin board downstairs."

She didn't bother to tell him if they had a crisis, they'd make him leave. No sense borrowing trouble.

The surgery room was a buzz of activity in preparation for the cesarean section delivery.

Annabelle's gaze automatically honed in on Zach's.

Oh, Lord, those dimples were going to be the death of her virginity. Good night, where had that thought come from?

She found herself blushing. Dr. Zachary Beaumont, not one to miss a trick, noticed and frowned.

Guiltily, she jerked her gaze away and focused on her job, her adrenaline surging as though a patient had just coded in front of her.

Darn it, she had to calm down. She was normally competent and composed, a rock in a crisis. That's what put her in such high demand with all the doctors.

The anesthesiologist was standing by, as was April Sullivan-McCallum, the neonatal nurse who also happened to be Maggie's sister-in-law. The atmosphere in the room was tense, yet everyone was putting on a good front.

Annabelle couldn't let everyone be thinking about bad memories of a thirty-one-year-old heartache—Emily McCallum's loss of life in childbirth.

By dog, that was *not* going to happen here. Not on her watch.

She went to the tape player and switched on a soft, toe-tapping rock-and-roll cassette.

Maggie glanced over. "Oh, that's my favorite. I play it for the babies all the time."

"Then they'll be anxious to get here and do a little dancin'," Annabelle said with a grin. "Although you ought to be ashamed for not starting them out early on honky-tonk tunes."

Maggie gave a weak laugh and grasped her husband's hand. He was gowned and standing next to her.

Zach gave her a slight nod of approval for her quick thinking, and she felt a thrill of excitement at his acknowledgment. She knew he could work under any circumstance. Even if she'd blared heavy metal music, it wouldn't distract him. He was a totally focused man. More so than necessary at times, Annabelle thought.

"Okay, Maggie," Zach said. "This is what we've been waiting for." He held her hand while Annabelle started an IV and hooked up numerous tubes and monitors.

Zachary Beaumont could appear unemotional, even harsh at times, but that wasn't his true nature. After working with him for the past eight months, Annabelle had come to realize that he was fiercely protective and had an excellent bedside manner.

When it came time to deliver babies, though, he was focused and dynamic—a "do something or get out of my way" kind of guy.

"I should have stayed in bed longer," Maggie said to Zach.

"Probably wouldn't have helped. This is very common with multiple births. Roll over toward me. Adam, give your wife a hand."

Once Maggie managed to shift to her side, Zach took her hand again, careful of the IV. "Let me give you a rundown on what to expect so you'll know what's happening. There's nothing to worry about. I've done these hundreds of times. Dr. Lee is going to give you an epidural so you won't feel anything with the birth. The epidural is going to be a bit painful, so hold on to Adam."

When Dr. Lee inserted the needle, Maggie gasped and Adam winced. "A *bit* painful? Dammit, Zach." She panted. "It's awful."

"Breathe through it, Maggie," Annabelle said, laying a hand on Maggie's leg, stroking. "That's right, almost done now."

Maggie continued to glare at Zach.

He grinned, and Annabelle didn't think that was the wisest choice he could have made. A woman getting an epidural would likely deck him—heck, the size of that needle even scared *her*. Thank goodness both of Maggie's hands were being held—by Adam as well as Zach.

He'd probably planned it that way, the devil.

"Don't let all these monitors and wires upset you," he continued. "They're so we can keep a watch on your and the babies' vitals. Annabelle's going to insert a catheter and have you drink a concoction for your stomach acids.

Then once we're ready to go, I'll make a vertical incision in your abdomen, as well as a uterine incision. I'll break the bags of water the babies are in and pass them over to April and her team of nurses. We'll let you see the babies, but they'll have to go to the NICU—''

"The what?" Maggie asked.

"Neonatal care unit," April Sullivan-McCallum said.

"Oh, that's right. I knew that."

A special twinkle appeared in Zach's eyes, a smile that didn't curve his lips. She'd noticed it countless times, and Annabelle thought it was one of the sexiest expressions she'd ever seen.

"I should have the babies delivered in ten minutes or less. Then all that's left is to stitch you up and move you to recovery."

"When will I get to see the babies? Hold them?"

"The pediatrician will be checking them over while you're in recovery. We'll arrange for you to go in a bit later." Zach glanced around the room, making sure everyone was in place. Annabelle nodded to let him know she was ready.

"Okay, any more questions? Maggie? Adam?"

"Just do a good job," Adam said.

"I always do."

The touch of arrogance in Zach's tone wasn't rude. It simply conveyed unequivocal confidence. And at a time like this, that level of confidence was soothing.

Annabelle handed him instruments by rote. They worked well as a team, and she'd assisted in so many of these births, she could probably do it on her own—not that she'd want to.

She noted that Adam was pale, holding his wife tenderly. It did her heart good to see that. The years of miscarriages and trying to get pregnant had taken a toll on their relationship. The love between them was evident, though. They were true soul mates.

She hoped the birth of these babies would bring them closer together once again. Though they would have a long haul ahead of them caring for five infants.

True to his word, Zach was in and out within nine minutes. "We have a girl," he said, holding her up and glancing at the clock. "Five thirty-one p.m. And she's already complaining." He passed the squalling baby to April, and Annabelle gave him an arch look for his sexist comment.

"This one's a fine-looking boy," he said a minute later. Two more boys and another girl were lifted up for Maggie and Adam's inspection, then quickly passed to the neonatal team, who suctioned and weighed the babies.

"We've got weights of five pounds one ounce, five pounds even, four-fourteen, four-thirteen, and another at four-thirteen," April announced, her voice filled with an aunt's pride and excitement even as her movements were efficient and quick.

"Why isn't the last girl crying?" Adam asked.

"She probably didn't like to be last and is holding her breath." The baby emitted a weak cry, and everyone breathed a sigh of relief. Then April and her team whisked the babies away to the NICU.

"Are they all okay?" Maggie asked, staring at the door.

"They're beautiful," Annabelle said. "You did great, Maggie. My gosh, think how wonderful you'll feel now that you're not carrying around twenty-five pounds of babies."

"Oh, I never looked at it that way."

"Mmm." While she talked, Annabelle automatically handed Zach instruments, anticipating before he could even hold out his hand for them. "It hurt me just to watch you try to get up out of a chair."

Maggie laughed, her whole body trembling. "Adam had to help me. I couldn't manage on my own."

Adam was rubbing her arms to warm her, soothe her. "I love helping you. Anytime I can get my hands on your skin, I'm a happy man."

"All right, you two," Annabelle said as Zach finished the last stitch. "Don't get carried away. You've got another six weeks before you can be foolin' around with each other."

"Killjoy," Adam said, but he kissed his wife anyway. The love between them was nearly tangible. They had each other, and now the family they'd so desperately wanted.

Something Annabelle desperately wanted.

A lump formed in her throat, and she looked away— right into Zach's solemn gaze.

She realized he'd been watching her, and when he noticed the tears hovering on her lower lashes, his rich chocolate eyes went so incredibly gentle, she nearly sobbed out loud.

Whatever passed between them in that one moment was new.

Something she couldn't quite describe filled the air, as though the successful birth of the quintuplets had forged a special bond between them. She felt a pull of attraction, of mutual respect, of curiosity, of awareness, that hadn't been there before.

What in the world was going on here?

A nurse wheeled Maggie out of the surgery room, and Adam stopped to pump Zach's hand, thanking him profusely.

After the high emotions of all that had transpired in the

surgical room began to subside, Annabelle felt a pang of distress. She'd raised her siblings and worked around babies all day, watching the miracle of birth. Yet each day a nagging worry assailed her.

The car accident that killed her mother had injured Annabelle, too. An unexpected infection in the hospital had cost her one of her ovaries and created scar tissue on her Fallopian tubes. Her periods weren't regular, and getting pregnant would not be an easy task. Her chances were extremely slim.

She yearned to settle down. To fall in love. To have a family of her own.

But would she ever find a man who would take her without guarantees? Flaws and all?

Her college boyfriend hadn't wanted to. And the wounds from his rejection went much deeper than the internal scars from the accident.

She should have learned her lesson from Peter. And she shouldn't be lusting after Dr. Zachary Beaumont.

"Deep thoughts?" Zach asked, startling her.

She laughed to cover her turmoil. "It's a failing of mine. I go off into daydreams and forget there's a world around me."

"Doesn't sound like a failing to me. Everybody needs dreams—day or night or long-term. Those dreams get us where we want to go."

"Did you always dream of being a doctor?"

"Yes. Always."

She gave him a bright smile. "Single-minded, are we?"

"Absolutely. I go after what I want."

She sucked in a breath. Surely he didn't mean...her? Good night, the intensity in those deep brown eyes was enough to make her melt right there on the spot.

Her heart pumped, and she couldn't have broken eye contact if somebody had shouted Code Blue.

Then, as though he hadn't just looked clear into her heart and soul, he swung an arm around her shoulders and headed her out of the surgery room.

"You did a great job, Annabelle. I always know I can count on you. What do you say we go talk to the family and let them admire and praise our skills?"

"Nothing wrong with your ego," she remarked, wishing he'd remove his arm. She was entirely too young to have heart failure.

And she had a sudden and horrible feeling her heart was definitely in danger—and had been since the day Dr. Zachary Beaumont had accepted the position at the clinic.

ZACH WASN'T SURPRISED when he walked into the waiting room and saw that it was filled to capacity. Adam must still be with Maggie, helping her settle in recovery, because the minute he and Annabelle cleared the doorway, everyone jumped up and flocked to them like worried hens.

Jackson McCallum led the pack. He was fifty-eight, with salt-and-pepper hair and a razor-sharp business sense that Zach appreciated. Zach admired anyone who was disciplined and exuded confidence. Aside from that, Jackson McCallum had donated the special wing that Zach worked in at Maitland Maternity.

"Maggie? Is she all right?"

Annabelle moved forward, easily slipping her arm around Jackson, offering her special brand of comfort. Zach had seen her do it countless times. There was a special quality about her, an easiness that drew people, soothed them.

"She's right as rain, Jackson. You have five healthy

grandbabies, although they'll be in NICU for a while yet. We can't say how long. Two girls and three boys. Good-size babies for being early.'' She rattled off their weights.

That was a female thing, Zach decided. He'd heard the nurses giving the weights, but he didn't recall the specifics of each baby, or which one weighed which. Annabelle knew right down to the sex.

She amazed him. He knew she was young—twenty-three. The youngest one at Maitland Maternity, but not immature. Just the opposite. He often forgot their age difference. She was the most efficient nurse he'd ever worked with, always one step ahead of him. It was uncanny how she finished his sentences and handed him instruments before he could even form the words to ask.

So, what the hell had just happened back there in the surgery room? He'd looked at her, *really* looked at her, and he hadn't been able to break the contact.

Her blond hair was streaked with highlights, her soft Texas drawl reminding him of a bluesy sax traversing a range of emotions that left the listener spellbound, hanging on every note.

And her smile. Why hadn't he ever noticed how it lit up not only her face, but those incredible green eyes? She radiated a confidence and joy that were hard to resist.

She was competent, serene, sexy and…fun.

Dammit, he was just tired. He wasn't attracted to Annabelle Reardon.

And that was a bald-faced lie.

The truth was, he didn't *want* to be attracted to her. She was way too young for him. His work was his life. He didn't have time for relationships. Oh, he dated. But the women he dated were only looking for a wealthy doctor to show off on their arm. Eye candy. A term usually reserved for a woman. But that's pretty much what he was to the women he escorted to fancy see-and-be-seen places.

Annabelle wouldn't be interested in a casual, shallow relationship.

She was the nurturing type who would want home, husband and babies. And that wasn't his gig.

"Let's go over to the Lone Star steak house and celebrate with a round of drinks," Madeline Russell suggested. She was the fertility specialist on Maggie and Adam's case, and she'd recently gotten married. Since he hadn't attended the wedding, he didn't know any of the particulars.

There were changes since her marriage, though. She was softer, more feminine, had stopped wearing those oversize tent dresses that hid her figure. And she wore her long black hair flowing down her back, not scraped into a matronly bun or tight braid. Happiness and a womanly confidence that comes from sex and knowing you're loved glowed on her face.

Man alive, it seemed love was in the air with half his colleagues taking the matrimonial walk down the aisle. Had someone put something in the drinking fountain at the clinic? Just in case, Zach decided he'd bring bottled water from now on.

Voices buzzed around him, and everyone enthusiastically agreed that a celebration was in order.

"I'm not sure I can make it," he said. He usually made it a point to keep his distance from his co-workers.

"Oh, come on, Zach," Annabelle said. "All work and no play isn't good for you. You were part of the team. One drink won't kill you."

Yeah, but watching Annabelle all night, with her bright smile and shining green eyes, might.

Chapter Two

Annabelle stopped by the NICU unit before she left to join the others at the Lone Star. Beepers screamed constantly, indicating that a baby might be having a crisis, and nurses hurried to check. The kids were impossibly small but perfectly formed, the equipment around them enormous.

April McCallum was tending to the quintuplets with her usual innate experience, all the while giving instructions to the nurses who would take over when she left. Every time Annabelle came into the unit, she was impressed by the efficiency, by the awesome miracles that came about in this very room.

They'd had babies in here weighing less than a can of green beans. She was continually awed by April's skill in changing minuscule diapers. And it was indeed a skill.

She stopped beside April, smiled at the quints who were sprawled in little isolettes equipped with oxygen hoods, their incredibly tiny bodies hooked up to monitors and wires and IVs. They weren't wrapped tightly in blankets like most newborns. Instead, they wore only tiny diapers, their chests bare to accommodate all the monitoring apparatus necessary to insure their progress in adjusting to their new world.

Such a shame that kids this tiny had to fight so hard for life.

"How are they doing?" she asked.

"Good," April said. "For preemie quints, they're big babies, which gives them a leg up. They'll be here for a while, though."

Which would be difficult for Maggie and Adam. Each day, Annabelle saw parents leaving the hospital with their arms empty, watching with sad, fearful faces as other proud, joyful parents happily whisked their newborns through those same doors, carrying flowers and balloons and struggling with car seats.

She'd seen them trying not to stare, imagined that they were happy for the other couples but perhaps wondering if that joyous day would ever come for them. Would their tiny, premature babies with underdeveloped lungs and other problems ever make it out these doors? Annabelle could hardly comprehend how parents could go through so much turmoil.

"How did you do it, April?"

"Do what?"

"Leave your four babies here every day and go home alone? Without them?"

April sighed and smiled. "It nearly tore my heart out. But since I work here, I got to see them more often than most parents."

Eight months ago, when a teenage mother had given birth to quads, the girl had known she couldn't care for four sick babies and had left them at the hospital with a note begging April to adopt them. April had fallen in love with those children on sight, as though they'd come from her own womb. When Matthew, the smallest, had been kidnapped, she'd been absolutely distraught until the baby boy was safely back in the hospital.

All had ended well. April and Caleb McCallum were happily married, and the adoption of the quads—two identical boys and two identical girls—was nearing the final stages. They'd even accepted the birth mother into their lives, proving what an incredible capacity they had to give love.

Annabelle dragged her gaze from the quintuplets and focused on the nurse. "Speaking of spending time in the NICU, what are you doing here? I know darn well you quit after you took the babies home."

"I promised Maggie and Adam I'd be here for their babies. My own little brood are in good hands, being spoiled by their aunties."

Annabelle smiled. "So are you going to take advantage of the night off and join us at the Lone Star for a celebration drink?"

"I hadn't heard about the plans."

"Madeline just suggested it in the waiting room. Caleb was there and he didn't object."

"It would be nice to have my husband to myself for a little while. Does that sound awful?"

"Of course not. You need a break every once in a while. Even if you only stay for one drink, you should come."

"You talked me into it. If Caleb agrees, we'll be there with bells on."

"Great. I just love a big party."

"Will Zach be there?"

Annabelle looked away, focusing on one of the kids. "Um, I think so."

"He was just in here a minute ago, right before you came in. He didn't say anything about going."

"Actually, he was trying to get out of it. I think I persuaded him otherwise."

April grinned. "Figured you would."

"Oh, stop. There's nothing going on between us."

"I have eyes, girl."

Annabelle turned toward the door. "Yeah, well, you better go get them checked then. I'll see you at the Lone Star."

"I'll be there…with my twenty-twenty vision."

Annabelle groaned. Was she that obvious? This wasn't the first time her friends had teased her about Dr. Zachary Beaumont. She'd have to watch her step.

After changing clothes, she made her way downstairs to the front exit of the hospital, waving to the receptionist as she let herself out the glass doors.

A blast of warm air swirled around her as she left the air-conditioned interior of the hospital. She'd walked to work this morning, and stopping at the NICU prevented her from hitching a ride with anyone to the Lone Star.

That was fine, though. The restaurant was just down the street a ways.

Enjoying the balmy August air, she headed along Mayfair Avenue, threading her arms through her backpack purse. Now that the sun had gone down, the awful humidity had abated somewhat. Still, her cotton tank top clung to her body, and her jeans felt like damp heat magnets. At least the restaurant would be cool.

She glanced up when a flashy Mercedes cruised by.

Zach's Mercedes. The tinted windows prevented her from seeing if he had anyone with him.

Her pulse elevated, and her steps picked up a bit. Why was she so obsessed with him lately? She'd been working with him for eight months and had managed to control her crush. Now, every time she handed him an instrument or met his dark brown eyes over the surgeon's mask, her knees went weak.

She'd never been a silly girl, given to fantasizing about men, but Zachary Beaumont had obviously jump-started her libido—even though he hadn't given her the slightest indication that he might be interested.

Except with that heated eye contact they'd made after delivering the quints. But that could have been her imagination.

And why would he be interested in her, anyway? Hospital gossip linked him to a different society girl every other week.

Still, she was having more and more difficulty corralling her fantasies lately. Which was ridiculous. Despite the attraction, the man had three strikes against him right off the bat.

He was a doctor, on call, and would never be home. Like her father hadn't been all those years until Jolene came into their lives. Annabelle wanted a man who would come home to her every night, be committed to her instead of the job.

Next, he didn't have children of his own. After her fiasco with Peter, she realized that most men eventually wanted babies to carry on the family name. At least that's what Peter had made her believe. She'd made it her goal to meet a man with a ready-made family. Then if she got pregnant by some miracle, it would be a bonus rather than an expectation.

And the third strike was—he was out of her league. Zachary Beaumont was champagne, caviar, five-star restaurants and Mercedes coupes. Annabelle was beer, burgers, backyard picnics and old Ford pickups.

But, even though he wasn't right for her, the man made her heart flutter and her knees turn to pudding.

ZACH WASN'T SURE why he let everyone talk him into a celebration. It was that sweet, sassy smile on Annabelle's face, he realized.

He'd told himself he'd have one drink and call it a night. He had plenty of medical journals waiting at home that he needed to read, charts to review, questions to answer on the Internet Web site he'd designed.

But each time he got up to leave, Annabelle's laughter would drift across the room, or her curvy body would be gyrating on the dance floor with one man or another—sometimes with a group of women, even. She had a verve that he found refreshing, a verve he imagined only the young possessed.

God knows, he'd lost that energy years ago.

She glanced at him, caught him watching. Instead of looking away, some devil inside him made him hold her gaze. He knew how to draw a woman to him with a mere look.

He saw her falter, hesitate, then that brilliant smile spread across her face, and a blond eyebrow lifted with such blatant, deliberate sensuality, he drew in a breath, cursed himself for letting his baser instincts get the better of his logical mind.

She excused herself from the dance floor, snagged a beer bottle off a nearby table and sauntered to his table, her tight jeans and even snugger tank top outlining every curve of her body.

Man alive, she made him want in a way he hadn't in more years than he could remember.

"Hey, there, handsome. How come you're sitting here all by yourself?"

"I was just getting ready to leave."

She sat down across from him. "Oh, don't be tellin' stories. You looked pretty rooted to that chair to me."

"Maybe I liked the scenery."

She opened her mouth, closed it, then laughed and took

a swig of beer. "For a minute there, I though you meant me."

"I did." His voice was deep and low, nearly drowned out by the music. Nearly.

He grinned because he'd rendered her speechless. That didn't normally happen to Annabelle Reardon. She could talk a baby right out of the womb.

"Well, then…uh, thank you for the compliment."

"You're welcome."

She laughed again. "Zachary Beaumont, stop baiting me. I'm not one of your curvy models who's impressed with your title and money."

"No? Tell me, then. What does it take to impress you?"

"Oh, things like loyalty and commitment."

He'd figured as much. "You don't think I possess those qualities?"

She shrugged. "Maybe you do. Your track record doesn't speak well for the image, though."

"Why is it everyone knows so much about my track record?"

"You're handsome and single, Zach. Certain people have made it their business to find out."

"You?"

"Heavens, no. I don't pry into others' lives. Now if they want to share with me, I'm happy to listen." She grinned. "You want to share?"

He couldn't help it. He laughed. "I think I'll keep my air of mystery."

"Darn it."

He lifted a brow. "Foiled your talk over the coffeepot, did I?"

She sobered at that and gave him a straight look.

"There's one thing you ought to know about me right now. I don't break a confidence and I don't gossip. I'll discuss what's common knowledge, as long as it's not gossip or won't harm the other person."

He reached across the table and laid a hand on top of hers. It was smooth as silk, her nails short and clear of polish.

"I already know that about you, Annabelle. I was teasing you."

She turned her hand beneath his and gave a squeeze. "Too much beer. I didn't mean to come off like a hornet. I can usually tell when someone's joking. Sorry."

The feel of her hand beneath his poked at an ache inside him that he wanted to ignore. Looking around the room for anything to take his mind off the feel of Annabelle's smooth skin and innate compassion, he focused on Madeline Sheppard-Russell and her new husband.

"I've noticed quite a change in Madeline in the past several months. She's more…"

Annabelle grinned. "Feminine? Happy? In love?"

"I guess. I'm not used to seeing her with her hair down. Who would have guessed it was so long—and that she had a figure?"

Taking a swig of beer, Annabelle said, "I get to take a little of the credit for the figure. April and I took her shopping and updated her image. Got Ian's attention, that's for sure."

"Ian would be her husband?"

"Where in the world have you been, sugar? Did I only dream that you work with the rest of us?"

Zach was a little surprised at himself for asking about a co-worker.

"I've always wondered why you keep to yourself so

much," she said. "We've all been a part of each other's lives around here."

"It's easier if I stay detached. If I'm personally involved, it could cloud my judgment in a crisis. A split second's hesitation can mean life or death for a mother or a child."

"Has that ever happened to you?"

"No. I haven't allowed it."

"I think you're wrong about yourself. If you care about someone, you'd be even more focused. That's the way you are."

She was probably right, and for some reason, it bothered him that she could read him so well. "You hardly know me," he said.

Her smile lit her face, danced in her eyes, making her look even younger—sexier. What a contradiction.

"It's a gift," she said and flicked her streaky blond hair behind her ear in an absent gesture. "I study people, listen to them. The next thing you know, I'm offering advice and wanting to fix them."

"I'm not broken."

"Of course you aren't. A bit touchy," she said, giving him a knowing look with a lift of one sassy eyebrow. "Let's see. Who else don't you know about?"

"You're out to prove a point, aren't you? That knowing my fellow colleagues won't cause me to flub the next surgery?"

"How very astute of you—and after two drinks, no less." She pointed to the crystal glasses on the table, one with only melting ice at the bottom.

"It's club soda."

"You don't drink?"

"Not if I'm driving or on call."

"Good for you. I'm neither—driving or on call." She

took another swig of beer, using her thumb to catch a dribble at the corner of her glossy lips. "So, let's see, obviously you know Maggie and Adam's story because you've handled their case. And you were in on the investigation when the teenage mother of the quadruplets disappeared and left the babies in April's care."

He nodded.

"Caleb was a true hero, marrying April so she could get custody of the quads." She sighed, and her eyes went dreamy.

"That's why they got married? I thought it was a love match." He had no business encouraging her. He couldn't seem to help himself.

"Oh, it is. Definitely. We found out a while back, though, that in the beginning, they'd both tried to convince themselves it was merely an arrangement. When Caleb's sister, Briana, married Hunter Callaghan and had the triplets, Jackson started pressuring Caleb to do the same—marry, that is. Not necessarily have the triplets. Caleb figured he'd get his dad off his back and do April a favor in the bargain—it looked better to the social workers if there were two parents to adopt the quads. Neither one of them counted on falling head over heels in love."

"That seems to be in the air," he mumbled. "Or in the water."

"What was that?"

"Nothing." Zach realized that in addition to Annabelle's ability to talk with hardly a pause, she was also a good listener, because she knew practically everyone's life history—some of which surprised him. He wasn't sure he wanted to know this much about his co-workers.

She wasn't a gossip, though. Despite the green daggers she'd shot at him when he'd teased her, he *did* know that.

The information she'd imparted was common knowledge. He'd just steered clear of it as much as possible.

Contrary to her insistence otherwise, he still felt it wasn't wise to get personally involved in people's lives. He worried that soft feelings would cause him to lose his edge.

Because at the bottom of his soul, hidden by a front, ran a deep well of compassion. He hoarded that self-knowledge like a squirrel in a secret acorn patch.

Caught up in his thoughts, it was a moment before he realized the laughter he heard was coming from beside their table.

Flushed from dancing, April and Madeline hovered over them.

"Okay, you two," Madeline said. "You're having too much fun over here hiding in the corner. Get your tushes out on the dance floor."

Before he could object, April had him by the hand, dragging him and Annabelle in her wake and turning them to face each other.

Annabelle laughed and gyrated that sexy body in the too-tight jeans. "If we don't go with the flow, we'll cause a scene."

He'd barely picked up the steps of the fast tune when the music ended. Saved, he thought, then realized he was doomed when a slow, dreamy ballad started immediately.

Everyone on the dance floor took their partners into their arms, each having eyes for only their spouses. Nothing he could do but draw Annabelle close. He couldn't just leave her standing here.

The minute her body eased up against his, he knew he was in trouble. Big trouble.

But did he stop? Hell, no. Instinctively, he pressed

against the small of her back, brought her so close a written prescription couldn't have squeezed between them.

He suppressed a groan, rested his cheek against her hair. It smelled like fresh apples, made him hungry. Hungry for the woman, not food.

He felt her warm breath against his neck, her rapid pulse beneath his fingers. She was as turned on as he was. He knew the way a woman's body worked. And this woman's was working overtime.

As was his.

She leaned back to look at him. That pressed the lower half of her body harder against his. But she didn't ease up on the pressure.

She gazed at him with the innocence of a lamb, unknowing that she was about to be led off by the wolf.

Surely she wasn't that innocent. Yes, she was young. He kept forgetting that.

But no woman as sexy as Annabelle Reardon could remain chaste for this long. The aura of sensuality in her movements would drive men wild.

Come to think of it, he didn't know that much about her personal life.

"Are you seeing anyone?"

"Hard to see anyone else in the room when I'm lookin' at you, sugar."

"I meant, do you have a boyfriend or something."

"No. If I did, I wouldn't be plastered up against you."

No, she wouldn't. "Why don't you have a boyfriend?"

She held her body slightly away, stiffened a bit in his arms, shrugged. "I was engaged once. He decided I wasn't right for him."

"Why the hell not?"

Her smile was soft, knocked him right in the solar plexus.

"Thank you for that. At the time I was crushed. Then I realized he was right. We wouldn't have suited. He's married now, with two kids. This is really mean of me to say, but he dropped out of college and went to work at a fast-food chain, never really made anything of himself. His wife supports them."

"Then he did you a favor." He pulled her close again, knowing he shouldn't, unable to help himself. The feel of her body against his was becoming like a drug he craved. He told himself he was offering comfort—she really was better off without the jerk of a fiancé.

Zach had little respect for anyone who didn't have goals, didn't pursue them. If working his way up the ladder in a fast-food chain was a person's goal, then that was different. He could respect that, respect the hard work. But to put the burden onto a wife instead of making every effort to better oneself, well, that was pretty low.

"Definitely better off without him," he murmured into her apple-scented hair.

He lost count of how many tunes they'd danced to. The band had taken a break, and the jukebox played slow ballads.

Zach looked around, noticed that most of their party had left.

When the song ended, he stepped back, his ego soaring when he noticed the dazed look on Annabelle's face. She'd been as caught up in the body contact as he, and unaware of their surroundings.

"Everyone's leaving. We probably should, too."

"Yes. Good thing I walked. That beer's gone straight to my head." She laughed. "Either the beer or it's you. Oh, Lord. Did I say that out loud?"

He grinned. "'Fraid so."

"Guess I can't take it back, then."

"Guess not. Did you say you walked?"

"Uh-huh. I live less than a mile from here. I like to get the exercise."

"Not in the middle of the night, you don't. I'll drive you home."

"Zach, that's not necessary—"

He put a finger on her lips, watched her green eyes widen. "It's absolutely necessary."

And probably a big mistake. Because if he drove her home, he'd want to come in. And if he went in, he wasn't one hundred percent sure he could keep his hands to himself, wasn't sure he could remember that they worked together.

He had a personal rule about dating co-workers. It didn't work. And he didn't do it.

The battle waging inside him over breaking that rule was fierce.

Hell. He ought to be running in the other direction.

But he was too much of a gentleman to let a lady walk the streets alone at night.

ANNABELLE HAD ADAPTED a mode of bluffing around Zach. She joked with him, tried to make him believe she was tough and sophisticated. Inside, she was a mass of hormones and nerves.

And now she was in his luxury car, which smelled of leather and wealth, and he was taking her home. Should she invite him in for coffee?

Oh, Lord, her education truly was lacking in this area. And she didn't want him to know.

Especially after that dance. His body had stirred up her insides, scaring her with the force of her need. She'd never reacted this way when she'd danced with Peter.

What was the proper etiquette in a situation like this

when a man nearly knocked a woman's socks off, then offered to drive her home? Were there expectations?

Did she want there to be? *Yes. Absolutely.*

Oh, dear. She was a nervous wreck. But, by dog, she wouldn't show it. This was her chance to find out what Zachary Beaumont was made of. Heck, she might even decide she didn't like him in that way after all.

Uh-huh. And Earl Frankle's prize pig was going to hop a ride to the moon on the next space shuttle.

Chapter Three

"Um, do you want to come in?"

Zach stared at her for a moment, then shut off the car. It wasn't a conscious decision. He'd already decided he was going to drop her off and leave well enough alone.

Before he could change his mind, tell *her* he'd changed his mind, she was hopping out of the car, waiting for him on the small patio leading to her apartment.

"Big mistake, Beaumont," he muttered, but got out of the car, pocketed the keys and followed.

"Oh, this weather is murder on my poor plants," she commented as she unlocked the door and flipped on the light.

A profusion of flowers spilled out of colorful pots in her little courtyard. Inside, lush, thriving houseplants were everywhere. Rather than feeling cluttered, the apartment felt restful. Welcoming. His immediate impression was that this was the type of home where you could put your feet up, rest and regroup. Yet, in direct contradiction, it vibrated with energy.

"How about coffee?" she called as she made her way to the kitchen, flipping on lights as she went.

"Sounds good to me." He promised himself he'd only stay for one cup. The jolt of caffeine would get him through the Web site e-mails he needed to read and respond to tonight.

"Cookies?" she offered, holding out a plate. He'd noticed that she always brought in goodies for the other nurses and doctors. Everyone looked forward to her treats.

He also noticed that she was nervous, didn't quite know where to look.

"Annabelle?" He took the plate of cookies from her, set them aside.

"What?"

"Relax, okay? I'm not going to jump your bones."

She let out a sigh. "Even if I asked you to?"

He knew she hadn't meant to verbalize that, could tell by the swift intake of her breath.

He closed his eyes, unwilling to let loose the images created by her simple, sensually packed words.

"I think we should change the subject." Dammit, he'd never been so tongue-tied—or off balance—with a woman before.

"You're right. I'm sorry. I have a habit of blurting whatever's on the tip of my tongue. Let's blame it on the beer."

He grinned. "That single beer you nursed all evening is taking an awfully big rap."

"I guess it doesn't take much to loosen my tongue."

"That's because you're such a little thing." He gazed at her, deliberately crowding her, unsure of what devil had gotten into him all of a sudden.

"I'm not little!" She tilted her head back to meet his gaze. "I'm five foot five. It's just that you tall guys are so used to looking over the tops of our heads, you *think* we're little. And I have it on good authority that my body's a pear."

"A pear?" He stepped back, gave her room and gave himself a better view.

"You know, little on top and bigger on the bottom. My friends and I were just discussing this the other week."

His eyes traveled over her body. "Sorry. I can't quite see a pear." Her breasts, molded by the tight tank top, were a nice handful. Her hips, encased in tight jeans, were a siren's call for any red-blooded man with a set of eyes. She wasn't skinny like the anorexics he usually dated. She was healthy and incredibly sexy.

Now, he could certainly imagine she might *taste* like a pear—sweet and juicy. But look like one? No way.

"Trust me," she said. "I know what I'm talking about."

He dragged his gaze from her body lest he get himself in trouble. Best to drop that particular subject, too.

Flowers bloomed in pots over the sink, on the dinette table, and spilled off a baker's rack in the corner.

"Did you have aspirations of being a horticulturist or florist?"

She laughed and reached for mugs to pour their coffee. "Actually my mother ran a nursery when she and my father met. Dad, wanting to impress her, studied up on the romantic language of flowers. After their first date, he sent her lilacs, which means 'I'm falling in love with you.' When he took her to dinner with a diamond ring in his pocket, he gave her two roses that were joined to form a single stem. She knew instantly that meant, 'Will you marry me?' The flowers spoke for him. She was touched that he cared enough to research her world. She said yes, and he gave her the ring."

"A romantic man."

"Very. Let's take our coffee in the living room. These chairs are too hard to relax in."

He picked up his mug and followed her to the sofa. She kicked off her shoes, then sat next to him on the couch, curling one leg beneath her and turning so she could face him.

"My mom was the love of Dad's life," she continued as though there hadn't been a break in the conversation.

"Was?"

"She was killed in an automobile accident. Dad was driving, I was in the back seat. Dad and I ended up in the hospital, but Mom died at the scene. Dad recovered physically, but not emotionally. He was a pharmaceutical salesman and he started traveling extensively to try to outrun his grief. That left me at thirteen to raise my brother and sisters."

"That's a lot of responsibility for a thirteen-year-old. Especially since you'd just lost your mother. How old were your brother and sisters?"

"Carrie Anne was nine, Lori was seven and the twins, Stevie and Sabra, were four."

"A baby raising babies."

"We did all right. I think I was always an old soul. Some of the kids in high school called me a Goody Two-shoes, and I have to admit that hurt. My mom was gone, and I had responsibilities that they didn't. While they were going to dances and parties and proms, I was cooking meals, driving the girls to ballet lessons and cheering at soccer games."

She shrugged, shifted on the couch and set her coffee mug on the table. "I didn't mind, though. We were close. And doing for my family gave me a sense of satisfaction and fulfillment."

He studied her for a long moment. "That's all well and good. But what about you? If you always put others first, who takes care of you?"

"I do." She bristled a bit, and he reached out to finger a strand of her hair, gave it a gentle tug, let her know he wasn't challenging her independence.

She smiled at him then. "I like it when your eyes speak like that."

"Like what?"

"Now don't go frowning and spoiling it. You have this way of smiling with just your eyes. It's a sort of tenderness."

He snorted a laugh. "I'm the least tender person you'd ever meet."

"Ah, Dr. B. likes to lie to himself."

"I do not."

She patted his cheek, leaned forward and pressed her lips briefly where her palm had been. The caress was over before he'd even gotten the signal from his heart to his brain that his pulse had risen.

"Anyway, Dad remarried when I was eighteen. Jolene is a fabulous person. She's taken over now, and she's the best thing that's come into our lives since the accident. She's the mom we missed having all those years."

"That's a nice thing to say about a stepparent. Most kids don't welcome the intrusion." He could still feel the heat from where her lips had touched his cheek, leaving behind the slick residue of gloss.

"You'd have to meet Jolene. You talk to her for five minutes and you fall in love with her." She made herself a little more comfortable on the couch, inched a bit closer to him.

"So, now I've told you my life history, why don't you tell me yours."

"I doubt you've told me your *whole* life history."

"The major highlights. Don't stall. Do you have siblings? Parents? What made you go into maternal-fetal medicine?''

"Whoa, that's a lot of questions at once."

"You're a multi-task kind of guy. I think you can handle it."

It constantly took him off guard the way she read him so well. And he didn't think she'd let up until she got her way. It'd be easier to comply than to fight it.

"I have an older sister, Mitzy, who's married to an investment banker. They have three girls, nine-year-old triplets, Rachael, Ashley and Michelle.''

"Triplets? Oh, my gosh, how wonderful.''

"Yes, they are. When I was a third-year resident, Mitzy got pregnant. She's a diabetic, so that made the high-risk pregnancy even more complicated. Watching the team of perinatologists take over her care and deliver healthy triplets is what motivated me to take the extra two-year subspecialty training program in maternal-fetal medicine. It's a specialty, as you know, that can be heartbreaking or incredibly joyful.''

"Yes. And the fact that you recognize that tells me you're not as gruff as you want to believe.''

He gave her a pointed look. "Do you want to hear this or psychoanalyze me?''

She gave him a sassy grin. "I'll hush.''

"Ha! That'll be the day. My mom lives on the outskirts of Austin—she owns a flower shop.''

"You're kidding! Both our moms had the same passion.''

"Seems so. My dad died just before I went to college.''

"Oh, Zach. I'm sorry.'' She leaned forward again, rubbed her palm over his arm, his shoulder, stroking, soothing.

She was a toucher, an innate habit—or quality—that

came second nature to her. He didn't think she was deliberately radiating sensuality, but it was there nonetheless.

Her face was so close to his. He could smell the apple scent of her hair, see the shiny gloss on her lips. He wanted to kiss those lips, taste the gloss. Ever since she'd gotten him thinking about the sweet nectar of a pear, his mouth had been watering.

He circled her wrist with his hand, went utterly still.

Annabelle froze, her hand on Zach's neck. She'd only meant to offer comfort. But the intense look in his chocolate brown eyes suggested he was feeling discomfort. The sexual kind.

Oh, she didn't have any experience in the actual act, but she knew enough to recognize when a man was aroused.

Her heart began to pump. She was on her knees beside him, her breasts practically brushing his face.

"Zach?"

"I told myself I wouldn't do this. I don't think I can stop it now."

He released her wrist, slid his hands to her waist and drew her forward. Off balance, she sprawled ungracefully onto his lap, felt a moment of embarrassment that he would notice her inexperience and run like the wind before she had a chance to experience him.

He didn't dump her and run. He slid his hand along her hip, positioned her on his lap, laid her over his arm and kissed her with a skill that made her see stars.

He came by his reputation as a ladies' man rightly. This guy knew what to do with a set of lips. He nibbled, toyed, teased and aroused. He didn't demand entrance, didn't rush for the prize.

Seduction. That's what he was doing to her.

She reached for the back of his head, drew him more firmly into the kiss, turned in his lap and poured every drop of emotion and need and wanting into that kiss.

Her forwardness was like releasing a dam. Where before his mouth had been gentle, now it demanded. And she gave. Freely, willingly.

She felt his palm against the bare skin of her stomach, smoothing over her bra. The front clasp popped open and he was cupping her.

Annabelle moaned, arched into him.

"You are so responsive," he murmured, shifting them, pulling her shirt over her head, laying her down on the sofa cushions and fitting his body over hers.

She tore at his shirt, snatched it off his shoulders, reveled in the feel of his wide chest pressing against her bare skin.

When his hand slid down her belly to unsnap her jeans, to touch her where she ached, she arched against him, unable to draw in enough air. She felt dizzy, out of control.

"I've never...I mean..." She didn't know how to say what needed to be said. As aroused as she was, she was still scared. This man was worldly. She wasn't anywhere near matching him. She didn't think it would be fair to continue her bluff.

He raised up, pressing their groins more snugly together. Annabelle nearly lost her train of thought.

"You've never what?"

Her face flamed.

"Are you saying you're a virgin?"

All she could do was nod. She wanted him to show her what making love was all about, put out this fire burning in her belly and between her thighs.

Before she knew what was happening, he sat up, reached for his shirt.

Feeling vulnerable lying sprawled on the couch without her tank top, she made a grab for it, tugged it over her head, not bothering with her bra. Her nipples showed through the white cotton, but there was nothing to be done about it.

"Dammit, Annabelle, I'm sorry."

"For what?"

"I should never have started that. I'm too old for you, anyway."

"What?" She had an urge to smack him, but controlled it. "You're joking, right?"

"You're twenty-three. I'm thirty-six."

"And your point?"

He stared at her, speechless.

"Age is merely a number, Zach. It's the person inside that counts." And that was the man Annabelle wanted. How in the world could he consider himself older? He was young, athletic, handsome, fun.

"Do you find me immature?"

"No. But you've just admitted you have no experience with men. You should find a younger man to discover each new day life brings, not some workaholic who's already been there and done that."

"You're starting to make me mad. I think I can make up my mind for myself. I was the boss in my family for a whole lot of years. For your information, I got along just fine making decisions without mucking up my life too bad."

"Look, I'm trying to be a good guy here."

"Who the heck asked you to be?" She fired the words back. In a minute she'd have the good sense to be embarrassed by her bold arguing. Right now, she was simply annoyed—never mind that she'd already decided earlier today the man had three strikes against him from the get-go. That he wasn't right for her.

Maybe she *was* touchy about her age. She worked with people older than she was. But that didn't mean she had less experience, that she wasn't just as mature, couldn't handle whatever came her way.

As far as sex went, sure she was inexperienced. She'd told him so as a courtesy. And for crying out loud, a girl had to learn sometime.

"I wasn't asking for a commitment of marriage, Zach. What's the big deal if I've decided to give up my virginity? I wasn't the only one who was feeling a rush of chemistry on that couch. Surely we're both mature enough to have a no-strings kind of fling."

Zach ran a hand through his hair. "I wish you wouldn't say stuff like that."

"Like—"

"Blunt," he interrupted. "Whatever is on the tip of your tongue or your brain."

"You want me to be silly and beat around the bush and hope you read my mind? I raised four kids. If I didn't make my wishes known, we'd have had no firm ground to stand on. I don't want to try and read someone else's mind or expect them to read mine. So, I'm blunt. Works better that way."

He sighed, took her hand. "Sit down," he said gently, then sat in the chair across from her as though not wanting to test his control by being too close.

"I had a relationship once with a co-worker. It didn't work out and it made it impossible for us to see each other every day at the hospital. She ended up transferring to another hospital, and I felt bad. I promised myself I'd

never be put in the position of disrupting someone's life—
or mine—that way again.''

Annabelle silently agreed that was a fairly good policy.
She loved her job. If they took this relationship further
and it went sour, could they work side by side in the
multiple birth wing the way they did now? Would hard
feelings cause her to choose? To leave her job? Transfer?

Or suffer daily watching him, unable to have him.

Was she borrowing trouble? Setting herself up for
heartache?

Well, heck. She was getting way ahead of herself, here.
She'd worked with him for eight months and managed to
corral her crush.

''If you recall, I didn't ask for a commitment.''

Just sex.

Thankfully, she kept that to herself.

''I know,'' he said. ''I just think we should keep things
the way they are—friends. You're too valuable to me to
take a chance on losing you.''

Oh, my. That was the nicest thing anyone had said to
her in a long time.

She stood up and held out her hand. ''Okay, you win.''
For now. ''Friends?''

He took her hand, gave it a squeeze, his features relieved. ''Friends.''

Annabelle noticed that his gaze dipped to her lips. She
barely controlled her smile. When she'd been beneath him
on the couch, friends was *not* what she'd been thinking
about.

He was the first man in her life who'd truly awakened
her sexuality, tempted her.

And if she got her way once, just once, he would be
the man to teach her the wonders of making love.

Chapter Four

Annabelle brought in a plate of double chocolate chip brownies the next day and put them in the break room, smiling when the doctors and nurses swooped in to claim them.

Zach, holding a bottle of water, nodded to her and looked away.

Well, so much for an easy friendship, she thought. That kiss was going to get in the way.

"Brownie, Zach?"

"No, thanks. I had a late breakfast."

She raised a brow. Did he follow such a rigid schedule that he couldn't allow himself a bit of chocolate?

Or a no-strings fling?

Darn it, she wasn't going to think about that.

When he excused himself, she felt annoyance eat at her insides.

"*I* won't turn down your delectable goodies."

"Why, thank you, Brad. It's always nice to be appreciated." Brad Stallings was a second-year medical resident. Young, a divorced father of two, he was handsome, fun-loving and the biggest flirt in the clinic.

"I definitely appreciate you," he said, wiggling his brows and giving her a teasing once-over.

"I'll remember that when y'all are bossing me around in surgery. Speaking of which, I've got to go check the schedule."

The board showed three cesareans with her name beside them as the assisting labor nurse. The first case, she would be working with Zach.

After scrubbing in, she prepared the room for surgery, then went to escort the expectant mother down the hall, easing nerves and rejoicing with her over the imminent joy of finally seeing her babies.

Suffering from a sudden onset of pre-eclampsia, Mrs. Presser looked a sight with her swollen face, hands and feet. Her blood pressure had peaked dangerously, and Zach hadn't wanted to wait any longer. Thank goodness she was nearly full term. And what a shame that her husband was away on business and wouldn't be able to get here in time for the birth of their children.

Zach was waiting in the surgery room when she rolled the patient in. Unlike yesterday, there were no long looks or locked gazes. He was all business, practically ignoring her.

Fine, if that's the way he wanted to play it, she'd do the same.

She did her job, kept a watch on the vital signs, firmly and competently slapped instruments in his hands.

"BP is one seventy over one thirty. Do you want me to push magnesium?"

"Yes. And go with the beta-blocker. Twenty milligrams."

Annabelle had already prepared the expected meds. She'd done this so many times, it bugged her to have to ask permission to act. Then again, it was Zach's malpractice insurance at stake.

His expression never changed, but she could tell when

he felt the need to hurry, to get in and get out as quickly as possible.

Judging his body language, she stepped up her pace. They worked as a silent team. The surgery went off without a hitch, and they delivered two healthy baby girls.

For the first time that day, Zach actually looked at her, met her gaze. "Thank you. You did an excellent job, as usual."

She sketched an impertinent bow. "I aim to please."

The skin at the corners of his eyes crinkled in a brief spark of amusement that he masked so quickly, she wondered if she'd imagined it.

Then he went to the sink, washed his hands and left the surgery room, leaving Annabelle to clean up and stew.

She had two more deliveries to assist before she could confront him.

And she did intend to confront him. There was no sense in them walking on eggshells around each other.

As the morning wore on, Annabelle's mind spun, vacillating between exasperation and strategies of how to make things right. If there was one thing she couldn't stand, it was discord.

Leaving the surgical wing after the third successful delivery, she slapped the elevator button, rode up to the second floor and knocked on Zach's office door.

"Come in."

She was already pushing the door open. She didn't usually give the courtesy of waiting for permission to enter. Normally, she'd give a soft knock and poke her head in. The fact that she hesitated disturbed her.

He glanced up, and his hand tightened on his pen.

"This is ridiculous," she said.

"This is exactly what I was talking about," he countered, obviously on the same wavelength.

"For pity's sake. We didn't even do anything. I may not have a whole lot of experience in the sex department, but at least I know when I *haven't* had it."

He stared at her for a heartbeat, then stunned her when he laughed. The sound was wonderful, the deep dimples in his cheeks making her want to touch.

"You ought to do that more. Look at you, buried under paperwork." She noticed a case of bottled water behind his desk, lifted a brow. "Don't trust the fancy water in the cooler they deliver each week?"

To her amazement, his skin flushed. Zachary Beaumont was blushing.

He shrugged and stacked his papers, laying them aside in precise stacks.

She let the subject of water go for now.

"You know what you need?"

"No, but I'm sure you're about to tell me."

"What you need is a day off. In fact, I checked your schedule and I happen to know you're free tomorrow. I'm here to invite you to a baseball game."

His brows rose. "I don't think the Astros are playing at Enron this week, and I'm fairly certain the Rangers are in Cleveland. You planning to drive to Florida or Chicago?"

"You just leave the itinerary to me."

"Forgive me, but that sounds a little dangerous."

She grinned. "Come on, live a little, Doc. I promise you'll have a great time. I won't steer you wrong. How about I pick you up at your place at eleven?"

"I can come for you."

Gotcha, she thought. He'd as much as agreed.

"No. This is my treat. A friendly ball game. There's only one rule. No talk about kissing and sex."

He did that thing again with his eyes, where they smiled but his mouth didn't. "You're on."

"Great."

"Annabelle?"

She turned at the door.

"Do you want my address?"

She felt her smile stretch. "I may not participate in gossip, but I do hear things. And it just so happened I was riding shotgun when some nurses passed your house and pointed it out to me."

He shook his head. "No privacy around here."

She laughed. "See you tomorrow, Dr. B. Wear your sneakers."

Zach stared at the closed door and shook his head, his smile growing despite himself.

Now the little spitfire was telling him how to dress.

ANNABELLE DROVE her pickup through the open gates of the estate. At least he hadn't changed his mind and locked her out. The massive brick structure in front of her nearly took her breath away.

"Definitely out of your league, Annabelle. What in the world are you thinking?" Obviously with her hormones instead of her rational brain.

Her old Ford looked a little sad sitting in his grand driveway. As though in agreement, it stayed running when she switched off the key, misfiring and acting ugly.

"Come on, Sadie. Be polite. This is no time to show your tail."

The front double-door entrance opened, and there stood Zach. Oh, Lord, the man made her drool.

Wearing faded jeans, a body-hugging polo shirt tucked in at the waist and the requisite tennis shoes she'd insisted on, he was the epitome of every fantasy she'd ever had.

Good night, how could the man consider himself old—or too old for her? He was mouthwatering.

She swallowed hard and slid out of the truck—which thankfully had quit doing the carburetor boogie.

"I like a woman who's punctual."

"And I like a man in a nice pair of jeans."

He gave her a warning look.

"What? I'm complimenting your clothes. I didn't say a word about sex or kissing."

He grinned and shook his head. "Annabelle, I don't know if I've got the energy to keep up with you."

She gave him a blatant once-over, standing in front of him, her hands in her hip pockets. "I think you can manage. Ready?" She was dying to get a look inside that house but wasn't going to be so gauche as to ask.

"As I'll ever be." He leaned sideways, picked up a ball cap from the hall table, and Annabelle got a glimpse of black and white marble floors and a huge elegant chandelier dripping crystals high over a massive, grand staircase that could have been right out of the set of *Gone With The Wind*.

"I'm going to ask for a raise," she commented.

He looked at her, saw that she was admiring the house. "Investments," he said. "I've done well with them."

"Maybe you'll give me some pointers sometime."

"Maybe."

"Okay. Hop into Sadie. She was in a bit of a snit a few minutes ago, but I think she'll mind her manners now."

"You've named your truck?"

"Of course. She's an important part of my life and gets me where I need to go. She deserves a name."

"Why is it a she instead of a he?"

"Because she sometimes has bouts of PMS." She slid in behind the steering wheel.

Zach hesitated. "We could take my car."

Annabelle lifted a brow. "Too good to ride in my truck, Dr. Beaumont?"

He shook his head, chuckled. This beautiful whirlwind absolutely confounded him. Confused him. How many women did he know who drove an old Ford pickup that had a name and PMS, or who would turn down a ride in his luxury Mercedes?

Annabelle Reardon was one of a kind.

He got in on the passenger side and tossed his hat on the seat. She looked like a kid in her tight jeans, her blond hair in a ponytail sticking out of the back opening of the baseball hat on her head. Her T-shirt had the word "Bears" emblazoned on the front and back.

She reversed, then let out the clutch, and off they went. He didn't think he'd ever ridden in a three-speed manual-shift truck before. She double-clutched into third gear and they picked up speed, winding through the roads, heading toward the outskirts of Austin. The air conditioner barely blew out cool air, so they had the windows down, letting in the scents of alfalfa fields and hot tar.

For a while, he simply watched her drive, watched her tap her fingers on the steering wheel to the beat of the country-and-western tune fading in and out on the radio, her ponytail bouncing, both from her head bobbing and the ruts in the road.

He told himself not to stare at what else was jiggling beneath the logo on her shirt every time the tires hit a pothole. Maybe this hadn't been such a great idea.

"Are the Bears the team you're rooting for?"

"They're the team I'm *playing* for."

"Playing?"

"Sure. Rival pharmaceutical companies. We're actually the Teddy Bears—my dad's name is Ted. The other guys are the Wolverines."

"Hmm. I think I'll root for the Wolves. They sound more aggressive than the Teddy Bears."

"Don't you dare. I'll hand you a scalpel instead of a clamp in surgery Monday morning."

He grinned. "That's an empty bluff if I've ever heard one."

"Well…I'll think of something. We're here."

She tooted her horn, stuck her hand out the open window and waved. The truck coughed and sputtered after she shut it off. She admonished it, then slid out and was enveloped in a group hug.

Family members, he concluded. The resemblance was there. Father, brother, three sisters, and the petite brunette with the perpetual smile must be the stepmother.

He stood by the front of the truck, not wanting to intrude. He was close to his mother and sister, but they didn't display this kind of open, public affection. He felt an odd pang, as though he was missing something in life.

"Zach," she called when she'd disentangled herself from the group. "Come meet the family."

He hadn't been prepared for this. He'd thought they were going to watch a game with a bunch of strangers. Instead of strangers, her whole family was here.

This was sort of like going home to meet the folks. Exactly what he *didn't* want to do.

He moved forward and shook hands with Ted Reardon.

"And these brats—" she introduced them "—are my siblings, Carrie Anne, Lori, Stevie and Sabra."

The girls, fourteen to nineteen, he remembered, all checked him out, then gave Annabelle a thumbs-up.

Oh, man.

"And this wonderful lady is Jolene," Annabelle said, putting her arm around the slender, beautiful woman.

Jolene held out her hand. "Welcome to bedlam, Zach. I hope we don't scare you off."

"No, ma'am, I don't scare easily. I have nine-year-old triplet nieces. I'm used to bedlam."

"Oh, he'll do nicely," Jolene said.

Zach stiffened. These people were getting the wrong impression.

Jolene caught his look and laughed. "I was actually speaking of your physique, if I may be so bold. Our first baseman called yesterday with a sprained wrist, leaving our team a player short."

His gaze honed in on Annabelle, who stared at him with a perfectly innocent expression on her face.

Wear your sneakers. He'd been had.

"I haven't played ball in a lot of years."

"We're not talking pros, here, son," Ted said. "Although I'd hate like heck to lose to those Wolverines. They're too smug for their own good."

"Oh, we can beat them with our hands tied behind our back, Daddy," Annabelle said. She looked at Zach. "You'll fill in, won't you? Heck, Stevie and Sabra are only fourteen, and they're game."

She was trying to shame him or appeal to his competitiveness. She'd chosen the right dare. Because he was nothing if not competitive.

He slapped his ball cap on his head. "Let me borrow a mitt. Who plays second base?"

"Carrie Anne."

"Then until I work the rusty kinks out, we'll trade and she can handle first, and I'll be second." He didn't want the responsibility of missing a catch that would stop a batter from going past first base. He figured second would be less pressure, less chance of letting the team down.

''Already taking charge.''

''It's called zeroing in on what's important, solving a problem and following through. It's the best course of action.''

She saluted him, smartly touching two fingers to the brim of her cap, and jogged to the field.

To the pitcher's mound.

A pitcher? Now he *really* had to prove himself. He wasn't sure why he felt the need to compete with her, but he did.

Damn, that woman intrigued him.

After exchanging his polo shirt for a Bears T-shirt, he took his position at second base because they'd lost the toss and the other team was up to bat. During warm-up, he practiced throwing the ball and catching it when Carrie Anne fired it back. When the ball went to third, then to Annabelle at the pitcher's mound then immediately to him, he nearly missed it.

She had a good arm. His palm was burning plenty. He put some muscle behind it and fired the ball to the catcher. It went wide, and Jolene had to snatch her face mask off and dive for it.

Everyone looked at him as if to say, ''I hope you can do better than that, bud.'' He grinned and stared back. So the ball went wide. He was rusty. He'd get the hang of it, by damn.

He didn't get a lot of practice in that round because the other team only managed two hits off Annabelle. Both were pop flies that were outs. The other batter struck out.

He grinned when Annabelle licked her finger and brushed it to the seat of her jeans in a touch-me-I'm-hot gesture, then smacked hands with her stepmother in a high five.

Instead of lining up in batting order with the rest of the team, he jogged off the field and scooted next to Annabelle. "I'm impressed."

"Well, I hope to shout."

He sputtered on a laugh. "Weren't you the one maligning my big ego the other day? Seems yours is a pretty good match."

"See there? Something in common. I bet if we pay attention we'll learn we have even more in common."

"Annabelle," he warned.

"What? I didn't say either one of our off-limits words. But *obviously,* Zachary, you're *thinking* them. Behave and cheer me on. I'm up to bat."

He had some trouble keeping his eye on the ball and off Annabelle's sexy rear end. When the bat cracked, her family went wild, jumping and whooping. Sabra grabbed him and danced him in a circle, screaming in his ear. He swiveled his head, trying to keep his eye on the play, and began yelling just as loud when she kept running the bases, finally sticking at third. A triple. Pretty darn good.

"Isn't she wonderful?" Sabra asked, beaming.

"Yes."

"Are you her boyfriend?"

"Uh, no. We work together."

"Too bad. You're pretty cute."

She danced off, left him standing there feeling his ears burn.

CELEBRATING their five-to-two win, the Teddy Bears went for pizza. As the newest team member—and because he was dependent on Annabelle for a ride—Zach went along with them.

"You did pretty good, slugger," he commented when Annabelle swung a leg over the bench seat and sat down beside him with a pitcher of soda.

"So did you."

"I struck out."

"Only the one time. You redeemed yourself when you hit that grounder and brought me home. You got us the winning run."

"I guess I did." That perked him up a bit. Suddenly he was famished. The smell of garlic and pizza sauce filled his senses. When Annabelle turned her head to speak to her stepmother, her sassy ponytail whipped him in the face, carrying the scent of apples to mingle with the rest of the aromas in the room.

He sat and watched the interaction between Annabelle and her family, amazed at the love, the laughter, the easiness. There was no formality, no rules, no admonishments for bad manners or talking out of turn. It was a free-for-all, everyone vying to tell their story above the din in the already noisy pizzeria.

Zach had gotten so used to wealth, to four-star restaurants, to solitude, to a housekeeper and a cook.

The emotion that suddenly swamped him was loneliness. He'd never recognized it before.

Annabelle poured them each a glass of soda, patted him on the thigh. "Don't talk so much, Zach."

He shook his head, enchanted. Yes, dammit, he was enchanted.

"You know, that's the first time I've played baseball since I was a little boy," he admitted.

"You're kidding. You didn't play in high school?"

"No. I was too busy making money as a kid, and by the time I got to high school, there wasn't time for sports in between studies and the stock market."

"Good night, you played the stock market?"

"I was an enterprising young man. Actually, it all started with my paper route when I was ten. I made pretty good money but figured I could do a lot better if I had more than one route and hired a couple of kids to work them."

"Did your parents know you were running a business and investing in the market before you'd even reached puberty?"

"I was pretty close to puberty when I started trading. And no, I didn't tell them. I was afraid they'd stop me, and I was determined to amass enough money to pay for my education. I knew what I wanted to do with my life, knew it would be expensive, and I didn't want my parents to have to foot the bill for it. They were fairly well off, but not rich. And even as a boy of ten, when I got my first paper route, I wanted to make my own way."

"That took a lot of single-minded determination."

"When you reach for a goal, you go all out. No matter what it takes."

Annabelle scooted her soda on the resin-coated table, watching the watery ring that smeared in its wake.

She had a couple of goals of her own, but right now they seemed unattainable. Perhaps she should adapt to Zach's way of thinking.

But how did one go about thinking positively about a body that was flawed, a body that would likely never produce children, when children were what she wanted most in this world?

"You told me your dad died. How old were you?"

"Right before I entered college. That's the only thing that could have deterred me. I offered to put my plans on hold, stay home. I hated to leave my mom and sister at a time like that when we were all still healing. I felt like I was leaving them in the lurch. But they insisted I go.''

''And I'm sure they got along fine.''

''Yes. Mom's flower shop does well for her.'' He grinned. ''But I do have a tendency to think I control the universe.''

''That you do. Someday, someone's going to jerk that rug from beneath you.'' It would probably be a woman. And it would break Annabelle's heart to sit by and watch, knowing she wasn't the right woman for him, knowing she would never be able to offer him a whole, fulfilled life.

''Hey, slugger.'' He tipped her chin up. ''Where'd you go?''

''Daydreaming again.''

''Didn't look like a very happy one to me.''

She bumped his shoulder with hers, gave him a sassy smile. ''Maybe I was just trying not to break our rules.''

''*Now* who's thinking about it. Accuse me, will you,'' he said with mock indignation.

She laughed. ''Okay, we're even. Sheesh, you are so competitive.''

Zach was different today, more relaxed and teasing, more forthcoming. He'd opened up to her, given her a glimpse into the boy he'd been, the life that had shaped the man.

And with each word that passed through his sculpted lips, each smile and crease of that intriguing dimple, each gentle, teasing look from those deep brown eyes, Annabelle found herself falling. Falling into him.

Falling for him.

MONDAY AFTERNOON, Annabelle knocked on Madeline Russell's door, then poked her head inside.

"Do you have a minute, Madeline?"

"Sure, come on in. Paperwork. I hate it. I'd much rather be doing sonograms and telling happy couples they're going to be parents at last."

Annabelle sat in the chair in front of Madeline's desk. "That's sort of why I'm here."

"You're pregnant?"

"No! Heavens, no." She sighed. "You know my medical history."

"Yes."

"And the chances of me getting pregnant the normal way are slim, right?"

"Slim, yes…but not out of the question."

Annabelle smiled softly. "I'm okay with this, Madeline. You don't have to soft-pedal with me."

"I'm sorry."

Annabelle felt like her problem was a catch-22. If she were to actively try for pregnancy through the normal channels with a man, it would have to be in a committed relationship. Perhaps an older man? Someone who already had kids of his own?

That left Zach out.

Still, she wouldn't mind being a stepparent to someone else's children. Her stepmother was an excellent role model. Then if she got pregnant by some miracle, it would be a bonus.

But she had no prospects like that on the horizon, and that's why she'd impulsively shown up in Madeline's office this afternoon.

"What about artificial insemination or in-vitro fertilization? I still have the one ovary." Plus scar tissue on her Fallopian tube.

Madeline shifted her long black hair behind her shoulders. She wore a blue silk tunic over matching slacks. It was an outfit Annabelle had helped her pick out when she and April had insisted on giving their friend a makeover.

"Annabelle, you're in the industry and you know how the fertility process works. The chance of multiple births is high, especially in a case like yours. In order to give you the best odds, we'd have to implant several eggs, and even then there's no guarantee."

"I know the odds."

"And you know the risks, as well. Do you really want to tackle multiple babies as a young single parent? Or is there a man in your life I don't know about?"

"There's no man." And no, she *wasn't* sure she wanted to tackle this alone—though she was suddenly getting annoyed that her age had become such an issue.

Her shoulders slumped. "No. I don't want to go through this alone. But doggone it, Madeline, I desperately want to feel whole."

Madeline was out of her chair and around the desk in a flash, putting her arms around Annabelle.

The compassion was too much. The ache in her throat swelled, the scars from Pete's accusation bubbling up like a cauldron, ending in a sob.

Years of giving, of being strong, of losing her mother, losing her womanhood, poured out in a rush of emotions as her friend held her in her arms.

"I'm sorry," she said. "I don't cry."

"Shh," Madeline soothed. "I know you don't. We all lean on you because you're so strong. You just lean on me for a minute or two. We'll figure something out, Annabelle. We won't give up."

In the meantime, any chance she might have had to honestly pursue Zachary Beaumont for the long term was lost to her.

Lost in the uncertainty of her body's ability to perform as God had intended it to.

Chapter Five

Zach paused beside his car in the hospital parking lot, started to open the door, then pocketed the keys. Annabelle, arms crossed as though she was cold—when it was a muggy eighty-five degrees out—walked slowly across the asphalt lot heading for the street.

She looked like she'd lost her best friend.

He shouldn't get involved. Dammit, his life had been fine before he'd learned the histories of everyone around him. Especially Annabelle's. This was just what he'd been trying to steer clear of.

Involvement.

It only took a few ground-eating steps to cross her path. She jerked her head up, gasped. "You gave me a start."

"You seemed lost in thought. You okay?"

She shrugged. "Sure."

"Where's your truck?"

"I walked."

"Into exercise, hmm?"

"It's that pear thing."

He shook his head, glanced at her derriere. "I'm looking, slugger, and I sure don't see it. Come on, I'll give you a ride before you ruin a good thing."

She grinned. "Why, Zachary, are you complimenting my rear end?"

"Yes. And don't go making anything of it, either. A friend can comment on another friend's backside."

He draped an arm around her shoulders and steered her to his car, opening the passenger door and waiting until she was seated before jogging around to the driver's side.

He didn't have any business feeling energized just because Annabelle Reardon was sitting in the leather seat of his Mercedes in her tight jeans and tank top and looking like she belonged exactly there.

He started the car, then paused. Before he thought better of it, he said, "I'm due at my sister's for dinner. Would you want to come?"

"Oh, I couldn't just drop in as an unexpected dinner guest."

She'd given him an out. He should have taken it. But the forlorn look that had been on her face moments ago brought out his protective instincts. If she was upset about something, she shouldn't have to go home alone—to solitude. He'd done that often enough himself.

"Mitzy won't care. I'll call her on my cell phone and warn her, if it'll make you feel better. Besides, you made me have pizza with your family. You owe me."

"Are you saying it was a bad experience?"

"No. No, I enjoyed it. I liked your family. Owe was the wrong word. Turnabout is fair play is more like it."

"Ah, we're back to competition. You're still miffed that I hit a triple and you struck out."

"You forget I redeemed myself with that grounder to center field."

"So you did. I'd love to meet your sister and nieces. I was only going home to a bowl of cold cereal, anyway."

"Cereal. And you being a nurse. You need a balanced meal."

"Probably. I get lazy sometimes. Too pooped to cook."

He didn't have that problem. His cook prepared a meal every night. All he had to do was sit down and eat. Then someone else cleared the table, did his wash, changed his sheets, kept the house straight and clean.

In addition to working all day, Annabelle went home to chores and doing for herself. It made him feel good that he was taking some of her burdens away tonight.

He just wished he knew what had caused the light to dim in those expressive eyes. The desolation he'd seen when she'd looked at him in the parking lot had worried him.

She was much too gregarious, much too sweet, to slip into that kind of sadness.

Did he have something to do with it? He'd been busy today with rounds and a conference. Since he hadn't had any surgeries scheduled, he hadn't seen much of Annabelle. Had she thought he was avoiding her again?

He enjoyed her company. Too much.

Now the question was, could he be her friend without wanting to take it further?

SIPPING COFFEE in Mitzy's kitchen, Zach watched Annabelle play with his nieces. Without a qualm, she sat right down on the floor with the girls after dinner to play some card game he'd never heard of, breaking up arguments that erupted and laughing with them.

She had a quality about her he found puzzling and refreshing. She could play and be a kid, but there was a line no one crossed. Both authority and love radiated from her. Her brother and sisters were very lucky to have had her when they were growing up.

"You've never brought a woman home to meet us before," Mitzi commented quietly beside him.

"Don't go reading anything into it, Sis. She's just a colleague."

"You don't look at her like a colleague."

"She's too young for me."

Mitzi snorted. "I'm eleven years younger than Bill. You're talking to the wrong person about age difference. We've got a storybook marriage."

"That's different."

"How?"

He didn't know. "Let it go, Sis."

"You know, one of these days that stubborn 'I'm always right' penchant you have is going to come back to bite you in the butt. You're going to realize you've been so focused on doing what you think is right that you've lost track when the cause is lost. It's not the age difference you're worried about. I hope it's not too late when you figure that out."

"You through analyzing me?"

"For tonight. I reserve the right to nag you again tomorrow."

He chuckled and stepped into the living room.

"Okay, girls, let my surgical nurse go. She's got to get up early in the morning and help me deliver babies."

"Aww, Uncle Zach, please. Just one more game."

He kissed each girl on the head and ruffled their hair. "Nope, I'm not falling for that 'Uncle Zach, please' stuff. I'm heartless tonight. It's not even beating."

"Let me see," Michelle said, leaping up to put her ear to his chest. Ashley and Rachael crowded around trying to horn in and get a listen.

Zach wrapped his arms around the three girls and lifted all of them at the same time, eliciting shrieks and giggles.

"Help," he begged, looking at Annabelle.

"You look strong enough to get out of that yourself. Besides, you started it."

"I changed my mind. I've got a healthy heart. It's Annabelle who's heartless."

The girls all giggled, but still clung to him like monkeys.

"I'm forever rescuing the man," she complained with a laugh. "Come on, girls. Give Uncle Zach some sugar and let him get me home. We have teeny-tiny babies to bring into the world and we can't be blurry-eyed from lack of sleep or we might forget and leave one of them in its mama's tummy."

Amazingly, they slid down his legs, obeying immediately, kissing him, then running to Annabelle and treating her to kisses, as well.

"Uncle Zach wouldn't really leave a baby in somebody's tummy, would he?" Ashley asked.

"I'm pretty sure he wouldn't do such a thing. He's the very best baby doctor. But we shouldn't chance it, should we?"

All three girls shook their heads.

Affronted that she'd even suggest such a thing, Zach was slightly appeased when she complimented his doctoring.

"Thanks for letting me intrude uninvited to dinner," Annabelle said to Mitzy. "I know it was tacky, but your brother can be a bit stubborn when he sets his mind to it."

"A bit?" Mitzy laughed. "That's an understatement."

Annabelle winked. "Most of the time I'm a fairly good match for that stubbornness."

Mitzy gave her a direct, woman-to-woman look, knowing full well Zach was watching and listening. "Yes," she said softly. "I think you might just be a match for him." She reached out and hugged Annabelle. "I'm so happy to have met you. You come again, hear?"

"Thank you for the invite. I'd love to."

"You know, it's not nice to whisper," Zach said, giving his sister a dark look.

"We weren't whispering."

"Mmm," he murmured, and bent to give Mitzy a kiss. "Thanks for dinner, Sis."

He held the car door while Annabelle got settled, then went around to the driver's side. Cicadas sang in the trees, sounding obscenely loud in the stillness of the country. Zach rolled up the power windows, and the climate-controlled air-conditioning unit blew cool air against his overheated skin. The tightly sealed doors shut out the sound of the harmonizing insects as though he'd pushed the power-off button on a stereo.

Pitch darkness surrounded them. This far out in the country, there were no streetlights to illuminate the way. Only the beams of his headlights and the green and amber lights of his dash.

"How do you do that?" he asked when they were on the highway.

"Do what?"

"Get kids to mind you so well?"

She laughed. "Years of practice. I might look like a softie, but my sisters said I had a certain look that made them feel guilty as all get-out and they'd hop to because they didn't want to disappoint me—or find out what I'd do if I lost my temper."

"You have a temper?"

"I don't think so. I'm pretty easygoing. Fussing upsets me, so I try to steer clear of it—or find a solution to fix it before it gets out of hand."

"Sometimes arguing is healthy."

She shrugged. "It makes me a wreck."

"So, are you one of those people who says yes when they really mean no?"

"No…yes…" She sighed. "Sometimes. I enjoy doing for others, but I do have my limits. It's taken me a while to set them, but I've managed."

"Mmm, in your advanced years."

He saw her blond hair swing as she jerked to look at him. "I'll pit my fairly well-adjusted psyche against your set-in-your-ways stubbornness any day of the week."

"Okay. I take it back. You have a bite."

She laughed. "That's twice tonight you've accused me of being scary."

"How do you figure?"

"Keeping the girls in line and biting."

"Your point." He could practically hear her thought. *Competitive.* He smiled in the darkness.

He usually drove in silence after a date, tuning out the chatter of his seatmate as she talked about so-and-so's dress or gossiped about who was cheating on whom or the latest catty list of cosmetic-surgery touch-ups.

This wasn't a date, though. It absolutely wasn't. It was two friends having dinner at his sister's house. Still, Annabelle engaged him, made him laugh, made him come alive.

When he pulled up in front of her apartment, he suddenly flashed on the last time he'd taken her home. [text obscured] the slow, full smile on her face, she was rememb[text obscured] too.

She raised a brow. "Want to come in?"

He shook his head. Damn, but he liked [text obscured] got charts to review."

She opened the door and hopped out of the car, then taunted over her shoulder, "Chicken."

She didn't look back, but he knew she was grinning. He waited until she'd gone inside, then put the car in gear and drove away.

No one had ever called him a chicken. They wouldn't dare.

Yet Annabelle had just hit the nail on the head. He *was* chicken. Scared right down to his toes to be alone with her. She wrecked his self-control.

Nobody had *ever* wrecked his self-control. He hadn't thought it was possible.

A WEEK LATER, Annabelle was getting frustrated. Zach was out of town a lot, and when he was in the hospital, he was so busy, they hardly ever spoke.

She'd filled her free time with family and friends, but she was restless.

And she'd gone on a baking spree last night.

On her break, she went into the lounge. Brad Stallings looked up from where he sat, moaning over a bite of chocolate cake.

"You made this," he said, his hazel eyes filled with worship.

"Sure did. It's called Better Than Sex cake."

He groaned again. "Marry me and run away with me."

She laughed and sat down, trying to decide if she wanted to get a soda. One of the doctors was leaning into the open refrigerator, so she decided to wait.

Brad scooted his chair next to hers, his widespread knees nearly touching hers. "Seriously, Annabelle. I want to go out with you."

"Going out and marrying are two different things.
up your mind."

"I'll settle for dinner," he said.

She realized he was serious. It dawned on her that she'd never given Brad a chance because of the crush she'd carried in her heart for Zachary Beaumont.

What the heck, she thought. Zach wasn't budging from this friendship-pact thing. Might as well have a night out with a nice man instead of sitting at home pining.

Besides, Brad did meet her requirements. He had children of his own. He wasn't commitment shy even though he'd been divorced. He'd told her himself he was the homebody type, and his ex-wife had been the one who'd wanted to gallivant. He was young and good-looking. And they'd never lacked for something to talk about.

"Dinner sounds good, Brad."

"Great. Maybe I can talk you out of that Better Than Sex recipe."

The refrigerator door slammed, rattling bottles of soda. Annabelle looked up.

Right into Zachary Beaumont's dark brown eyes.

With a bottle of water in his hand, he nodded to them both and left the lounge.

Brad didn't seem to notice anything amiss.

Annabelle's adrenaline was pumping like a screaming heart monitor.

Darn him, acting like a dog in the manger when he'd been practically ignoring her. Was he jealous? *Well, hmm.* That could be advantageous.

She took a breath, decided to let the chips fall where they may. "What time?" she asked Brad.

"Seven o'clock? I'll pick you up at your place."

"Do you need the address?"

He gave her a sheepish grin. "I looked it up."

"Shame on you. I'll see you at seven."

ZACH HAD NEVER felt jealousy before. He didn't like it. This burning, gut-wrenching, vacillating between worry and anger, feeling sick at his stomach. His territorial, protective instincts were stirred up but good.

He couldn't keep his mind on anything but Annabelle out on a date with another man.

Dammit, she'd said she was ready to get rid of her virginity. He'd done the honorable thing and politely declined—and been taking cold showers ever since.

So, was she going to give it to that wet-behind-the-ears medical resident? Hell, the guy couldn't even stay married for more than five years. He had no sticking power, obviously didn't value a woman, believe in till-death-do-us-part.

Zach drew up short. Did *he* believe in that? His parents had had it. His sister had it. Annabelle's dad had found it twice.

He paced the study, oblivious to the computer monitor flashing that he had e-mail, the massive bookshelves filled with medical journals and paperback fiction, the open files on his desk.

"Okay, Annabelle," he said aloud. "You win. If you're so all-fired determined to learn about making love, it's *not* going to be with that smooth-talking octopus you're having dinner with." He snatched his keys off the hall table.

"Give me the recipe for Better Than Sex cake," he mimicked. "Yeah, right. All the better to taste you, my dear, said the wolf to Red Riding Hood." He snorted. "Not with my lady, buddy."

ANNABELLE enjoyed Brad's company, but her heart just hadn't been in the date. Zach had effectively ruined it by hiding behind the refrigerator door—and invading her mind every five seconds, making it next to impossible to concentrate on her date.

Wouldn't you know. The man didn't want her. Then he spoiled her chance to test the waters on a potentially good thing.

Brad stopped the car in front of her apartment, put his arm over the back of the seat, toyed with her hair.

"Your mind was somewhere else tonight."

Appalled that it had shown, she apologized. "I'm sorry. I really did have a good time."

He smiled softly. "It was worth a try."

He glanced toward her apartment, and Annabelle stiffened, hoping he wasn't going to ask if he could come in.

"Pretty hard to compete with Dr. Beaumont."

"Where in the world would you get an idea like that?"

"Probably from Dr. B. himself, seeing as he's coming toward the car looking like he wants to bash my face in."

Annabelle whipped around. Her heart lurched in gladness. Then she felt bad for Brad.

"I'm sorry, Brad." She already had the car door open. Zach had stopped on the sidewalk, hands in his pockets.

"No need to apologize. I've seen you watching him. And I've seen him watching you." He shrugged. "Good luck, kid. You deserve it. If things don't work, though, I'll be around."

She leaned down at the window. "You're a good man, Brad."

"Get going before the guy has heart failure."

She smiled, straightened up and turned. Brad pulled away from the curb, but Annabelle didn't move for several moments. Neither did Zach.

At last she took a step, walked past him to the front door, her pulse drumming in her ears when she realized he was right by her side.

Unlocking the door, she looked at him. "What brings you here, Zach?" she asked softly.

"You." His voice was just as soft, with an edge that held a warning she didn't quite understand.

"What if I hadn't come home?"

"Then I'd have waited...or found you."

"Did you come here because you want me or because you wanted to protect my virtue?"

He stared at her, a muscle ticking in his jaw, his brown eyes intense.

She wasn't sure what got into her, why she felt the need to push him. "Maybe my virtue no longer needs protecting. Maybe we went to Brad's place."

The muscle still ticked in his jaw. "I don't think so." His voice was barely above a whisper.

"So sure of yourself, Zach?"

He slammed his palm on the door, shoved it all the way open. Before she could catch her breath, he had her in his arms, carrying her over the threshold, kicking the door shut, shooting the lock home.

"Yeah, I'm sure. You don't look like a woman who's been properly satisfied." His mouth came down on hers. She expected aggression, anger even. She didn't expect the incredible tenderness.

It knocked down every one of her defenses. She wrapped her arms around his neck, poured herself into the kiss. This is where she wanted to be. In Zachary Beaumont's arms. Lost in his kiss, his touch.

At last.

"Bedroom?" he asked, his voice unsteady.

"Second door down the hall. Hurry."

His steps were quick, but once he lay her on the bed, time seemed to still into slow motion. He gazed at her, sat on the mattress beside her, stroked her hair, kissed her gently.

"I'm scared to death," he said.

She gave a nervous laugh. "I think that's my line."

"I've never been anyone's first. Are you sure about this, Annabelle? Speak now, because once I put my hands on you, I don't think I'll be able to stop."

"I don't want you to stop."

"Then we need to establish some rules."

She groaned. "You're gonna mess up the mood, Zach."

"Then I'll just have to get it going again, won't I?"

He was so self-assured, she shivered. She was just talking out of nerves. She didn't think anything could ease the acute arousal she felt right now.

"The rules are, this time's for you. Watch me. Feel what my hands and body do to you. Tell me what you like and what you don't like."

"But I don't know—"

"You will. You will." He ran his hands over her, undressed her slowly, his gaze following every slow movement. Then he stood and removed his clothes, pausing, giving her a moment to gaze at his body.

Her heart pounded. She felt vulnerable, frightened, aroused.

Then he lay down beside her, took her face tenderly between his palms and kissed her. Just that. For endless moments he made sweet love to her with his lips and his tongue, worshiping, reverently, gently.

In light of his patience, she expected a slow building of desire. Instead, it flashed out of control. Her hands fisted against the sheets, lifted to touch his body, urge him.

He drew back, caught her hands in his, raised them

above her head. "Uh-uh. No touching. Or this'll be over before either of us is ready."

"I'm ready."

"For it to be over?"

"No, doggone it. For you to get on with things."

He smiled, released her hands, used the tips of his fingers to map her body. From head to toe he stroked her, found points of pleasure she had no idea existed. He was a doctor. He knew how a woman's body worked. There was nothing clinical, however, in the way he touched her.

It could have been hours. She lost track of time.

She was aroused to the point of pain, not thinking, forgetting the rules. She used her heel against the mattress for leverage, rolled him over, slid on top of him and gave in to her desire to feast. Her hands and lips were fevered. She didn't need experience to know what to do. She let her heart guide her.

Zach swore and flipped her over as though they were in a wrestling match—and perhaps they were.

"You broke the rules." His breathing was none too steady.

She opened her thighs, pressed her fingers into his buttocks. "I guess you better do something about it, then."

He tried to go slow, was nearly out of his mind with pleasure. He carefully entered her, paused when she stiffened.

"Easy." He pulled back, determined to be gentle if it killed him. She took the choice out of his hands, lifted her hips and met him with a force that made him swear, made stars burst behind his closed eyelids.

"Are you okay?" he asked when he was sure he could speak.

"Better than okay. Make love to me, Zach."

And he did. With everything in him he had to give.

Acutely aware of every breath and every moan, he gauged her mood, her pleasure, gave her more, holding on to his own control by the sheerest of threads.

He felt her surrender, felt the pulsing of her body around him, swallowed her climactic scream with his mouth as he let her ride the crest, then found his own release.

His heart was beating like mad when he suddenly realized he hadn't used a condom.

He shifted to his side, drew her against him. "Ah, hell, Annabelle, I forgot about birth control."

She stiffened for just an instant, then continued to stroke her hand over his damp chest. "I'm safe."

No one was one hundred percent safe. He should have been feeling concern. Instead, something had shifted inside him. He could picture Annabelle carrying his child—or his children.

Testing the waters—she was so strong he often couldn't tell where he stood with her—he commented, "You know, multiple births run in both our families. We could end up having that ourselves."

Annabelle felt panic engulf her. She hadn't told him about her flaw. She wasn't the woman for him.

She'd watched Zach with the children he held, watched how he interacted with her brother and sisters, how he'd responded to his nieces.

The grapevine claimed he was a confirmed bachelor, but she didn't believe it. There was a yearning in him that he probably didn't even realize existed. But Annabelle had seen it.

She was in over her head. Faced with having to confess her shortcomings—to a man she'd fallen irrevocably, totally in love with.

She sat up, holding the sheet to her breasts.

"Annabelle?"

She was trying to form a sophisticated quip when Zach's beeper went off.

He tossed aside the tangled sheets, strode naked to his slacks, checked the number, then picked up Annabelle's bedside phone.

"This is Dr. Beaumont. I got a page."

He listened for a minute, then started snatching clothes even before he'd gotten the phone hung up.

"What is it?" Annabelle asked, reacting to his urgency. She'd always been able to read him so well. After what they'd just shared in this bed, she imagined the connection was going to be even stronger. She wasn't sure how she would stand it.

"Car accident. Paramedics are bringing Layla Drummen directly to the clinic. She's in labor and bleeding vaginally."

Annabelle hopped out of bed and grabbed clean jeans and a T-shirt from her closet. "You'll need me."

"Yes. I *do* need you, Annabelle. And as soon as this crisis is over, we're going to talk about what's bothering you."

It was a threat, pure and simple. Zach wasn't a man who'd take no for an answer.

Chapter Six

Zach raced through the night. Both of them were silent as they rushed into the hospital. Since she lived so close to the clinic, they beat the paramedics there.

As they scrubbed up, Zach said, "Layla Drummen has an atrial septic defect. Usually women with this disorder are asymptomatic, like Layla's been. She's tolerated her entire pregnancy without cardiac complications. With the accident, though, I'm not taking any chances. She's thirty-one weeks. It's risky, but if we don't take the child, we won't save the mother."

The paramedics brought the gurney in on a run, shouting vital signs, briefing Zach on the injuries, telling him the patient had insisted on being brought to Maitland Maternity Clinic rather than the emergency room.

Annabelle hooked up monitors, prepared Layla for emergency surgery, her heart racing, wishing Dr. Lee would hurry up and administer the anesthesia. Cut and bleeding, there was no way this woman would have the strength to deliver naturally.

"Someone call ER and get the attending in here," Zach yelled over the noise. A nurse ran to the wall phone.

The heart monitor Annabelle had hooked up suddenly screamed, flat-lined.

Zach cursed. An eerie calm engulfed Annabelle even as she made snap decisions. Ingrained procedure took over.

She snatched the cesarean tray and thrust it within Zach's reach, slapped a scalpel in his hand, then kicked a stool next to the gurney to give her height and leverage and began manual CPR compressions, shouting to the mother. Until Zach got the baby out, she couldn't use the defibrillation paddles.

"Come on, Layla. Don't do this, dammit! You've got a baby coming into this world. Hold on for him." Her arms burned and shook from the exertion. Another nurse squeezed the oxygen pump. Where the heck was the ER doctor? "Come back to me, Layla."

The baby was out and gave a single, very weak cry.

"It's a boy, Layla. Fight, dammit. Come back." Her arms were fatigued, her throat going hoarse. "Open your eyes, look at your baby!"

At last the heart monitor beeped an unsteady sinus rhythm of thirty, then forty. Not great, but it would do.

She looked at Zach, at the baby who wasn't much bigger than his palm. He shook his head, shrugged, then handed the tiny infant off to the neonatal nurse who rushed it to NICU.

Despite the horrendous struggle that child would have clinging to life, Annabelle said, "He's beautiful, Layla. You did it, sweetie. Good job."

And Zach had done a good job, as well. He'd had that baby out in four minutes. That was excellent for the prognosis of the child, less time to be oxygen starved.

She stood back so the attending physician could check the rest of Layla's injuries and assisted Zach in closing the incision.

He glanced at her. "You're a hell of a woman, Annabelle Reardon."

His voice was filled with awe…and something that sounded suspiciously like love.

ZACH LOOKED for Annabelle in the lounge and frowned when she wasn't there. Something was wrong. He could feel it in his bones.

He headed toward the exit doors, saw her walking across the parking lot.

Dammit. He jogged to catch up with her, reached for her arm to stop her. "Hey, slugger. It's customary to go home with the guy who brought you."

"I thought you'd be a while, maybe want to stay and monitor Layla."

"I've done all I can. The rest is up to the internists and vascular guys. Besides, haven't we had this conversation before about you walking the streets at night?" He tried to tease, but it fell flat.

"I've been taking care of myself for a lot of years, Zach. I don't need a keeper."

He frowned at her tone. "What's going on, Annabelle?" He hadn't counted on the emotions that would swamp him when he made love with Annabelle. Like the door to a castle yawning open, letting out all the secrets and knowledge of the universe, he'd known in an instant what he'd been searching for all these years.

It wasn't work, or single-minded goals, or money and respect.

It was Annabelle. It was this enormous feeling inside him that filled him like the heat of surgical lights, bathing him in the glow of love, in a rightness that couldn't be denied.

"We had a good time together, Zach. But you're right.

It's not wise to get involved with co-workers. I think we should cool things down before they get out of hand.''

"Out of…they're already out of hand on my part.''

Annabelle drew in a deep breath, praying for strength. Grabbing at straws, she said, "What about that age difference you're always harping about? It won't work, Zach.''

"Do you really believe that?''

Her insides were twisted into knots. She couldn't hold on. Had to. But one look at the hurt expression on his face, and she crumbled. She shook her head, whispered, "No.'' The pain was tearing her up.

He put a finger under her chin, lifted her face. "I love you, Annabelle. I've never said that to a woman before.''

Oh, God. Tears burned, filled her throat, spilled over her lids.

"Oh, baby, don't.'' He drew her into his arms, held her. "Talk to me, sweetheart. Tell me what this is really about.''

They were alone in the parking lot, spotlighted by the mercury vapor lights. She wished she could say this in the dark so she wouldn't have to see the pity in his eyes.

"I don't think I can have children. The accident that killed my mom also did internal damage to me.''

He looked at her as though waiting for the bad part.

"Zach. You're a man who's made to be a father. Didn't you hear me? I can't give you babies.''

He frowned, clearly puzzled. "I don't remember asking you to. Still, look where you work, Annabelle. This job of all jobs—this place—should give you hope.''

"Yes, it gives me hope. But it doesn't give me guarantees. I could never ask you to enter into a relationship when having a child isn't a certainty. That's why I insisted on a no-strings relationship—''

"Relationship?" he interrupted incredulously. "I don't want a *relationship,* dammit. I want a partnership. Marriage. I'm not marrying a baby maker, I'm marrying the woman I love. The woman who's all I need."

Just like him to speak as though she'd already agreed.

"You're not listening," she said, but hope made the protest weak.

"No, *you're* not listening. You've had my life in turmoil since the minute I laid eyes on you eight months ago. Maybe this will get your attention."

He brought her right up on the tips of her toes and gave her a kiss that blanked her mind of everything, a kiss that was filled with promise, with hope, with a love so all-encompassing every last piece of her life fell into place like a completed puzzle.

"Now tell me you don't love me," he challenged.

How had she ever gotten so lucky? "Eight months?" she asked. "You've had a thing for me for eight months?"

"For every minute of every hour."

Happiness nearly brought her to her knees. "We're a couple of fools and we've wasted a lot of time."

"Annabelle…"

She knew what he wanted to hear.

"Yes, Zach. I *do* love you. I have…for every minute of every hour since you walked into Maitland Maternity with those sexy dimples and do-something-or-get-out-of-my-way attitude."

"And you'll marry me."

"It might be nice if you asked."

"I just did."

"No. You told me."

He took her hand, got down on one knee. Annabelle glanced around the parking lot, giggled. Zachary Beaumont wasn't the type of man to go for open displays in public—on dirty asphalt.

"Annabelle Reardon, will you do me the honor of marrying me? Be my wife, my partner and my love for as long as we live?"

Tears blurred her vision. She tugged at his hand. "Yes. For heaven's sake, stand up before security comes over here shining a spotlight on us."

He laughed, picked her up off the ground and swung her around. "That's one of the things I love about you. I know I'll never have a dull moment around you."

After he kissed her senseless, Annabelle pulled back. "Tell me something?"

"Anything."

"What's with the case of water in your office, the bottles you're always carrying around lately."

He laughed long and loud. "After the McCallum quints were born, I was noticing the difference in Madeline Russell and realizing that half our colleagues were taking the matrimonial walk down the aisle. I had this crazy notion that somebody had put a love potion in the drinking fountain."

"And now?" she asked.

"I'm throwing away my bottled water. Love had bitten me way before that, the minute you fixed those green eyes on me and held out your hand in introduction."

"Well, then, it's nice to know I've got such a potent touch."

"Oh, you do. Absolutely."

He drew her into his arms and kissed her, and Annabelle knew once and for all that what began that hot August night after their special delivery of the McCallum quintuplets was truly real.

A forever love.

And with luck, whether through natural means or medical assistance, someday they just might have their own very special delivery.

Because love was hope…and love healed.

AND BABIES MAKE SEVEN

Mary Anne Wilson

Chapter One

The first cry came at midnight, and before Maggie McCallum could open her eyes, another cry joined in with the first one.

"I'm coming," she muttered as sleep totally dissolved for her and she got out of bed in the master suite. She barely noticed that Adam wasn't in bed and didn't bother with her robe, heading through the shadows of the house in an oversize T-shirt Adam had worn in college.

"I'm coming," she whispered again as the cries grew in volume when she stepped into the hallway. There was little light, but she knew the way by heart to the renovated game room that had become the nursery for five babies. Her babies. And they were crying.

Those cries were echoing behind her from the monitor and in front of her, loud even through the closed doors at the end of the corridor. The nursery had been a vast game room in the single-story ranch-style house they'd moved into just before the quints came home from the hospital. But now it was a fully equipped nursery with everything the five tiny lives needed. Including a monitoring system wired directly to the master bedroom so Maggie could hear everything that went on in the room.

She pushed back the doors she'd painted with rainbows,

a symbol of the hope that the babies had brought with them, and went into the thirty-by-twenty-foot room. The idea had been to make the space peaceful, from the pale blue walls to the off-white ceiling and the deeper blue carpeting on the hardwood floors. But there was little peace with five six-month-old babies living in the space.

Grace Weston, the nearest thing Adam had had to a mother, was with the babies. She stayed overnight several times a week to spell the live-in help Maggie had, and she was wonderful, everything Maggie could want, but that didn't stop Maggie from going into the room and heading for the cribs that formed a circle in the center of the room. Five white cribs, all of them near the others and easy to get to, with five changing tables at their feet. The setup had taken on the look of a wheel, with the cribs the spokes and the three rocking chairs the hubs, while the changing tables made the outer rim. It worked, at least for now.

Grace was leaning over the nearest crib, talking softly, her voice almost drowned out by the crying. Maggie went to her, touched her on her back and said, "What's wrong?"

The tiny, gray-haired woman didn't look up from the crying baby, but motioned over her shoulder to the next crib. "I told you to turn off the monitor."

"And I told you I wasn't going to." She went closer and looked at baby Douglas lying on his back, the covers long ago kicked off and his tiny face scrunched up tightly as he let out another scream. "Is he hungry?"

"He's always hungry," Grace said, scooping up the tiny boy and cradling him against her shoulder. "He's a bit colicky, that's all. A bit of a bubble in his tummy." As she started jiggling him while she softly patted him on his back, the crying faltered a bit and became soft gulps. "Now I've got Master Douglas under control, and since you're here, my namesake seems to need to be changed." She nodded to the crib directly opposite them. "Why don't you do that?"

Maggie crossed to Gracie. As she reached for the little girl, she felt that familiar leap of her heart when she saw any of her children. Five of them. Tiny lives. Hers and Adam's. Five at the same time. She lifted Gracie, a decidedly damp baby at the moment, and thought about how much it had taken to get them all here safe and sound. So much worry and fear, and Adam having the added worry of knowing his mother hadn't survived the birth of himself, his sister, Briana, and his brother, Caleb. That was three babies, and they'd had five.

After three months in the hospital, they were all home and doing well. The last thing she could do when they started to cry was sleep. She cuddled a damp Gracie to her breast and whispered, "Gracie, girl, you are definitely wet." Remarkably, the baby quieted immediately. "Good girl," she said, putting the baby on the changing table and stripping off the damp diaper.

When the baby was changed, she picked her up and cuddled her. She turned to find Douglas in his crib, settling with a sigh while Grace stroked his almost bald head. Maggie glanced at the other babies, Jackson, Daniel and Julia, relieved that they had apparently slept right through their brother's and sister's uproar.

Grace came toward Maggie and slipped Gracie out of her arms. "Let me take the little one," she murmured, and the baby went to her without a murmur. Grace had raised Adam, loved him, and she loved the new babies. She helped all the time with the quints, but Maggie never quite relaxed, never quite had the ability to turn her back and let someone else do for her children.

Silence finally ruled in the nursery, and Grace eased the baby into her crib. Satisfied that Gracie was settled, she turned to Maggie and pointed to the door. Maggie took a quick look at all the babies, then followed Grace out of the room into the hallway. Grace closed the door behind them, then faced Maggie in the softly lit hallway. "I told you to turn off the monitor, that I was staying tonight to help Louise so you could get some rest, and so could Adam." She glanced down the hallway and lowered her voice even more as she smiled slightly. "That man could always sleep through anything."

Maggie realized then that Adam hadn't been in bed with her. His side hadn't been slept in at all. "He's not here," she said.

Grace frowned. "It has to be midnight. Where is he?"

She hugged her arms around her. "I don't know. Work, I guess. He…" She bit her lip. She couldn't remember what he'd said when he'd called earlier, because Julia had been crying. She'd only half listened, but remembered something about an affidavit that had been wrong. "You know how it is. He's snowed under at work. The Mc-Callum men don't seem to know when to stop."

Grace didn't say anything to that, but the slight shake of her head spoke volumes. Then she said, "You get back to bed. I'll stay in here for a while and read to make sure they're settled for now." She urged Maggie toward the master bedroom. "Turn off the monitor and call Adam at work and tell him to get on home."

"Thanks," Maggie whispered and headed for the bedroom.

She stepped into the shadowed room, glanced at the empty bed and wondered how she couldn't have noticed Adam hadn't come home. There had been a time when she couldn't sleep unless he was with her, even when they'd been under pressure to conceive. Even then, he was part of her, part of her soul. She slipped into the bed, far too big a bed for one person, and was about to reach for the phone on the night table when the door opened.

Adam. He strode into the room, and there was an instant connection that wasn't there unless he was close by. The jacket of his dark suit was gone, and his tie hung undone from the collar of a pearl gray shirt. Shadows touched the man, blurring his features, but she knew them by heart. The hazel eyes, sandy brown hair that was always a touch too long, spiked a bit from his habit of running his fingers through it when he was deep in thought. A faint dimple played at the left side of his full mouth. It seemed forever since she'd touched that dimple. "Hello and welcome home," she breathed, sitting back against the coolness of the headboard.

He hesitated in midstride, but kept going as he muttered, "Thanks." There was an edge to his voice that made her tense. He walked quietly past the bed to the huge walk-in closet. A flash of light came, then he was out of sight in the closet, which was the size of a small bedroom.

"Adam?" she called. "Why were you working so late?"

"I told you on the phone, the Rhyder deposition," he said, his voice vaguely muffled in the distance. "It won't die."

She wrapped her arms around her bare legs, resting her chin on her knees as she stared hard at the open doors of the closet. "Can't someone else take care of it for you?"

There was no response for a moment, then Adam was back, all his clothes but his jockey shorts gone. They were vividly white against his tanned skin, and she swallowed hard. Dark hair formed a faint V on his chest, disappearing into the waistband of the shorts. ''Probably, but I'm doing it.''

She jerked her eyes up, startled that at the moment she was feeling decidedly like a hormone-driven teenager. For months, it seemed, the pregnancy and babies had overridden everything, but, at that moment, she wanted her husband with a hunger that was startling to her. ''It's so late,'' she said, her mouth slightly dry. ''I was worried.''

He was by the side of the bed, his side, and too far away from her. ''Did you need something?''

For some reason, she couldn't just say, ''I want you.'' It would have been so simple before the pregnancy problem got in their way. ''I just…I was thinking…'' She bit her lip hard.

He made no move to get into bed. ''What were you thinking?'' he asked in a low voice, and she cursed the shadows, wishing she could see his eyes, see what he was thinking.

She shrugged. ''About…things,'' she stammered, feeling more than a bit foolish. She was suddenly very embarrassed to be looking at her husband with such lust, at his lean and tanned body that belied his hours behind a desk.

And he was near naked. ''Things?''

''Important things,'' she blurted, wishing she'd had time to put on some makeup and wasn't wearing an old T-shirt instead of a sexy nightgown.

He came around the bed, standing directly over her, and she jerked her eyes up to meet his gaze. She loved him beyond words. Really loved him. And she almost forgot what it felt like being loved by him. ''What's wrong?'' he asked. ''Sniffles, fever, diaper rash?''

''What?'' she asked, disoriented for a moment, then she shook her head. ''Oh, no, no. Just fussiness. Grace thinks that Daniel might be starting to teethe, but I think he's too young, and premature babies sort of lag behind the others.''

He held up one hand. ''Enough. If you weren't thinking about the babies, then what? Are you feeling okay?''

She looked at her hands pressed to her bare thighs. ''I'm okay.'' She bit her lip as she met his gaze again. ''Oh, Adam, I was just…just…''

He hunkered down in front of her, not touching her, and she ached to be touched by him. ''Oh, baby, what is it?'' he asked, his voice low and soft and just for her.

Tears were there, coming from nowhere, stinging her eyes. ''I don't know.'' She bit her lip hard to keep it steady, then blurted, ''I miss you.''

He was still for what seemed forever. His exhale was a rough rush of air around them. ''I'm here,'' he whispered in a slightly unsteady voice, then touched her. His fingers lightly brushed her cheek, sending a shock of awareness through her, making her take a short gasp. ''Right here.''

''We never…hardly…anymore, I mean…''

''I know, love, I know.''

''The babies, I love them so much, and there's so much to do, and you and I…we…''

''You need more help. You need to trust Grace and the others to be there, to care for them, and you need time.'' His hand on her trembled. ''God, we need time.''

She ached for what had been between them at the first. ''We'll have time, when they're older and okay. They're so tiny and so fragile.''

His touch was gone abruptly. But he stayed close. ''Maggie, my love, we don't know how much time we have, and if we can't figure out how to have us in the middle of all of the baby stuff, I don't know what to do.''

It had seemed so simple to Maggie. Fall in love, get married, have children, live happily ever after. But it hadn't been that way. The loving had been easy, and the marriage had been wonderfully perfect. The children had been the hard part. She'd never dreamed she wouldn't just get pregnant, that they couldn't just love each other and make a baby. There had been months of testing, treatments and anxious lovemaking—at the right times.

Eventually, they'd had a miracle happen, fivefold. Grace, Douglas, Jackson, Julia and Daniel. And their lives had been changed more than she'd ever dreamed possible. Three months of going to the hospital four times a day, giving breast milk for the babies, holding them when she could or standing by their incubators. And Adam had been there with her all the time. Adam, as solid as a rock. Understanding that she was exhausted, that she was worried, that she had to get to the hospital first thing in the morning and go last thing at night. That she'd had nightmares about something happening to one of the babies.

Then the quints had come home, and the days of the hospital had seemed serene and calm compared to the reality of fitting five little babies into their lives.

"We can do it," she managed to utter. "We'll figure it out."

He exhaled. "Get more help and step back a bit. Take time to just be Maggie."

Maggie. Maggie loved this man. And Maggie was aching for this man. She looked right at him, and this time she touched him, barely cupping his chin with her fingers and feeling the slight bristle of a beard against her skin. "Maggie knows that all five little McCallums are asleep for the moment, and Grace is in the nursery, and..." She trailed her hand down to his bare shoulder, then lower to press her palm against his chest. She felt his heart beating, felt each breath he took. "You're here, and I'm here."

"Why, Mrs. McCallum, are you trying to seduce me?" he asked, his voice rumbling against her hand from deep in his chest.

"I think so. I'm a bit out of practice and this old T-shirt isn't black lace…"

"Then we'll take care of that," he said softly, and in an easy motion tugged at the cotton and slipped it off. "Better than black lace."

Adam loved Maggie. Simple, very simple. And in that moment, he'd never loved her more. There was no black lace, just a woman who was beautiful beyond words. A woman who had cut the long hair he'd loved so much into a shorter than short feathery cap, and he'd hidden his disappointment when she'd explained how much simpler it was with the babies to have short hair.

But right then, she looked incredibly lovely. Her face was thinner, her eyes more pronounced from dark shadows that lingered there, her lips full and inviting. Her breasts were heavier, fuller, the nipples darker, and her waist wasn't as narrow as it had been, her hips rounder, but she had never been sexier to him.

He went closer, cupped the weight of her breasts in his hands and felt the response, the tightening of her nipples, a small shudder, then a sharp intake of air. All they had was now, and he wanted her. His body tightened with anticipation, and he slipped off his shorts before he eased her back on the huge bed, into the coolness of mussed linen until he was over her.

It seemed an eternity since they'd been together because they both wanted it, because they both craved it. He felt her softness and her heat. His response was instantaneous and almost painful. Her arms were around his

neck. Her hips lifted to him. There was no gradual building to this point. There was a raw urgency between them,
a need that had been there for so long that Adam didn't
know when it had started.

He felt her, tested her, then entered her, and in a flash
of pleasure, he felt whole. As if he'd been broken and
lost, then been healed and found. He moved in her, felt
her rise to meet him with each thrust. Her legs were
wrapped around his hips, keeping him in her. As he
moved in her, the feelings flooded through him, filling
him, overwhelming him, and for that moment in time, it
was all right. Everything was all right.

Until a cry pierced the softness around them, then another cry mingled with it, and when Maggie froze under
him, he knew it was the beginning of the end.

"Oh, the babies," she whispered, motionless, and lowered her legs. He didn't dare move, because if he did, he
knew he'd take her, and he didn't want it to be this way.

"They're okay. You said Grace is there," he whispered, kissing her quickly and hard against her soft lips
before he drew back. He prayed that she would accept it,
that she'd stay right here.

But when he saw her face in the shadows, he knew. He
felt his heart sink. She eased away, whispering, "It's Gracie and she's been fussy all night, and maybe it is teeth."

How she knew the cries of one baby from another always stunned him. But right then, he didn't care. She
framed his face with both her hands. "I'm sorry, sweetheart. I'm really sorry. I'll…I'll be right back. I promise."

He didn't want her to go. He wanted to scream and
force her to stay, but he rolled to one side and didn't look
as she got out of bed. His arms were empty and the air
around him was cool, almost cold on the dampness on his
skin. He looked at her as she grabbed the T-shirt and

tugged it on. "I'll just check," she said, then climbed on the bed, and for an instant he thought she was teasing and wasn't leaving.

Until she was over him and kissing him quickly, then drawing back. "Save my place."

"Let Grace do it," he said before he could stop himself.

"They need me, their mother," she said, hesitating. "You know how I feel, that I want to be there for them… always."

He rolled away from her and sat on the side of the bed, with his back to her. His body ached with his need of her, and he didn't do a thing to hide it. "And you're going to make damn certain you'll never be like your mother."

"That's not fair," she muttered from behind him. "She walked out on me long before I even understood. That's over. I'm doing what I want to do, what I've always wanted to do, just love my babies."

"And you do. But you need help. You can't do this all alone," he said, twisting around, but she was going, halfway to the door.

Then she was gone, the door closing behind her, and he was alone. Again. He reached over and flipped off the monitor, shutting off the cries, and he fell back on the bed.

He ached physically from being so close to Maggie and being denied. He ached emotionally from feeling so isolated. It was there, that old desire and need. Something he'd tried to repress since Maggie had started to spot early in the pregnancy. Just holding her and loving her had been enough for a very long time, but it wasn't now. He wanted more, and she wasn't there to give it to him.

He rolled onto his side, got out of bed and headed for the bathroom. The discomfort in his body was nothing compared to the discomfort in his soul, and when he stepped under the hot water in the shower, he shivered. He couldn't be losing Maggie. He couldn't be. But somewhere deep inside, he knew he was.

Chapter Two

Maggie hurried to the bedroom after helping Grace settle the baby, but Adam wasn't there. She heard the shower and thought of going into the bathroom and climbing in with Adam. But she was so tired. She thought she'd lie down for a bit, wait for him to come back, then take up where they'd left off.

So she climbed into bed, reached for his pillow to pull it to her chest. Hugging it, she listened to the running water. She closed her eyes and imagined him in the shower, the water streaming over him, and the idea of joining him was there again. The idea of touching his sleek body, of having him run his hands over her, was so tempting. She'd go in, she thought, she'd surprise him, and that was the last thought she had until morning. Someplace between her idea and the act of getting out of bed and doing it, she fell asleep. Then Grace was there, touching her shoulder.

She squinted at the older woman who had the ability to look remarkably fresh even after a rough night, then twisted to see the clock, shocked that it read almost ten o'clock. She shoved herself to a sitting position, felt the empty spot beside her when she pressed her hand flat on the sheet to balance herself and knew Adam was long gone. "What's happening?"

"You've slept most of the morning away, sweetie, and I was starting to get worried."

She sat straighter, sleep falling away completely. "The babies—?"

"They're fine, just fine, but I was a bit worried when you slept through our morning course of cries and feeding."

"Oh, shoot, I'm sorry," she said, scrambling to the side of the bed to sit up and rake her fingers through her hair. She'd never slept through the morning production before.

"Oh, I'm not complaining. I think you needed the sleep, and Adam said not to wake you up."

"Adam? When…when did he leave?"

"Early, maybe eight o'clock."

She'd slept through everything, and she was so angry at herself she could spit. "I guess I was really tired," she muttered, standing to stretch and get her bearings. "I don't know how I could have slept through the babies crying."

"They were unusually loud this morning. Must be teeth, the way I figure it. They aren't usually so fussy."

"Maybe I need to turn the monitor up," she said, turning to reach for the volume switch on the monitor by the light on the nightstand, then stopped. The red light wasn't glowing. It wasn't on. She reached for the button, pressed it in, and she could hear Louise in the nursery singing "Twinkle, Twinkle, Little Star" in a painfully cheery voice.

"How did it get turned off? I wouldn't have—" She bit her lip as she remembered the way Adam hated the monitor and wanted her to turn it off. "Adam turned it off."

"And you needed the break," Grace said, crossing her arms over the blue housedress she was wearing. "He's a good man, Maggie."

Grace worshiped Adam. There was no way Maggie could say what she really thought right then. So, she settled for saying, "He's sneaky," then turned and looked for her robe. She shrugged on the white terry cloth and did up the belt. "Are the munchkins okay?"

"I told you, they're doing fine. I just came in to tell you I'm heading off home. Douglas needs some things, so I'll be back tomorrow sometime. Meanwhile, Louise is here, and you know you can call me any time you need me, no matter what?"

"Sure, and thanks for last night."

Grace glanced at the monitor, then at Maggie. "Thank your husband," she said and, with a smile and a nod, left.

"I'll do that," Maggie said, then sank down on the bed and reached for the phone. She dialed Adam's private number, and it only rang once before he answered. "McCallum here."

"Well, McCallum, this is Mrs. McCallum."

"Good morning. Sleep well?"

"Why wouldn't I, when you turned off the monitor?"

"Did I do that?"

"You know you did, and I wish you hadn't. You know I need to have it on. I can't just turn it off like that."

"After last night, I think you should."

"The babies were only up twice last night," she said.

"It only took one time to—" He took a deep breath, and she could hear him exhale roughly. "Sure ruined it for me."

"I told you to wait for me."

"I was in the shower, and when I got out you were sound asleep."

"I'm sorry." She felt heat in her face at the memory of what she'd wanted to do but had obviously been too tired to do. "I heard you and I thought I'd wait for you."

His voice lowered to an intimate level. "You could have come in to get me so I knew you were there."

"You could have woken me," she countered.

"You were too tired. And I have to get back to work."

"I'll see you tonight?"

"I guess so, if the babies sleep and you don't." Before she could say anything to that, he added, "Have a good day and kiss the babies for me."

The line clicked, then buzzed. She looked at the phone, slowly hung it up and whispered, "I love you."

ADAM STAYED at the office until almost eleven o'clock and was ready to leave when the guard from the front desk called and told him he had a visitor. For a minute he thought it was Maggie coming to get him. He'd called earlier and spoken to Louise. Maggie had been busy rocking Jackson, so he'd left a message not to wait up for him, that he'd be late. Then he'd hung up and dug into work, anything to make him forget for a while how disjointed his life felt lately.

"Your father's on his way up," the man said on the phone.

"Thanks," Adam murmured and hung up, shocked that the old man would be anywhere near the business section of the city at this time of night. He was usually at his mansion, as far from here as he could get.

Adam sank back in his swivel chair in the beige-on-beige office, pushed the stack of papers away and waited. He knew his dad didn't just visit. There was something going on.

Jackson McCallum barely knocked on the outer door

before striding into the office. Adam saw a fit man of fifty-eight, dressed conservatively in a dark suit that set off his thick gray hair. A man who had lost himself in his work when Adam's mother, Emily, had died, he was a different man now. Work was still there, but he was also a doting granddad to Caleb's quads, celebrating the finalized adoption of the babies, and then there was Brianna's triplets. The man had a full life, never seeming to take a moment to breathe, but he seemed happier then he'd ever been before.

Adam stood as the older man came into the room. As always, he wasn't quite sure how to react to his dad's presence. The softening in his father hadn't extended to him exactly. What should he do, shake his hand? Smile and nod? Hug him? No. He did the usual, by simply saying, "Dad? Good to see you."

Jackson nodded, crossed to the desk and looked at Adam. "I thought you'd be here." He glanced around the cluttered office, then his hazel eyes met Adam's gaze. "I'm afraid I was a bad teacher," he said on a sigh as he sank down in one of two leather chairs that faced the desk.

Adam took his seat and leaned back. "How so?"

"You don't know when to work and when to go home," Jackson said, looking decidedly grim as he spoke. "Took me years to figure that one out."

"I'm busy," Adam murmured, not willing to go home to an empty bed and a wife so exhausted she couldn't think straight. "Lots to do."

Jackson and Adam had never been really close. In fact, Adam had probably been closer to Douglas, Grace's husband, who'd worked as Jackson's chauffeur for years until his retirement a few years ago, but he'd always known his father was there. That he was proud of him in his own way. But Adam always thought his father had never stopped grieving for his mother, that grief had occupied most of his mind and soul. When his father spoke again, he realized how much the older man cared and how much he understood what was going on with his son.

Jackson looked around the office, shook his head when he glanced at the wall clock, then looked right at Adam and said, "You've got no right being here. You're losing her."

Adam was shocked by his father's words, but he didn't have to ask, "Who?" or "What do you mean?" He wasn't going to give any defense for being here and not at home. His father knew what he was doing. "I don't want to do that," he admitted.

His father looked almost pained. "Then don't let it happen."

"What can I do? How can I rip her away from those babies?" He stopped. He didn't want to do that, just to have her the way he had before. Just the two of them for a moment in time.

"You love her, don't you, son?"

"You know I do."

"Then tell her. Show her. She needs it as much as you do, and if you let it go, maybe there won't be another time." Jackson grimaced. Then whatever he was thinking about was gone, and he stood to look down at Adam. "Your babies are a downright miracle, the way you and your brother and sister were and still are. And their kids…" He shook his head in wonder. "God, miracles. But so is having that one person who loves you and you love. That one person who fills your life and…" He'd stopped, then exhaled roughly. "Get away for a few days together, and remember why you started all this in the first place. Maybe go to the cabin at the lake. It's empty and it's private."

"I wish we could," Adam murmured.

"Don't wish for it, just do it. Grace will be there for the kids, and you can be there for Maggie. You make it happen with your wife. Just do it."

Adam looked at Jackson and felt closer to his father then he ever had in his life. "Okay," he said and meant it. "I will do it."

Jackson nodded, and without another word, he left. As the door shut behind him, Adam reached for his coat. He was leaving, too. He had a lot of thinking to do and some calls to make.

MAGGIE DIDN'T KNOW when Adam came home. She'd fallen asleep, and he hadn't tried to wake her. She only knew that when she woke to the cries in the morning, around seven o'clock, his side of the bed was mussed but empty.

She got her robe and headed for the nursery, surprised to find Grace there with Louise. After the morning rituals of feeding, bathing, changing and holding, Louise stayed with the babies while Maggie and Grace headed down to the kitchen for coffee.

"You're here early," Maggie said to Grace as the two of them walked into the kitchen at the back of the sprawling house.

"I had things to do, so I thought, since I was up and around, I'd come on by for a while."

As they stepped into the cavernous kitchen, Maggie looked at Grace. "Did you see Adam this morning before he went to work?"

Grace crossed to the white ceramic counter, heading for the coffeemaker with its glowing red light and stack of heavy mugs by it. "He didn't go to work," Grace said as she poured coffee, then turned with the mugs in her hands and motioned with her head toward the breakfast room at the rear of the kitchen. "Let's sit and talk for a bit."

Maggie didn't argue. She had a sense that something was up, but she didn't have a clue what it could be. The babies were fine—a bit fussy, but safe and sound in the nursery. But Grace coming in early like this wasn't usual. And if Adam wasn't at work, where was he?

Maggie crossed to the glass-topped table, sank down in a wicker chair and reached for the mug Grace held out to her. "Yes, I think we need to talk," she said before she took a sip of the hot, strong liquid.

She set the mug on the tabletop as Grace settled in the chair across from her. "First of all, what do you mean, Adam isn't at work?" she asked.

"He didn't go to work," Grace said before taking her own sip of coffee.

"Then where is he?"

"He's in the den. Said he was going to make some calls, last I heard."

Maggie cradled the warm ceramic mug in both hands. "He has lots of work to do. He didn't get home until very late last night...I think. I just assumed, when he wasn't there this morning..."

"You assumed what?"

She was startled by Adam's voice coming from behind her. The coffee in the mug sloshed slightly but didn't spill. Turning, she saw Adam striding into the breakfast room. He wasn't in his suit and tie. He wore a pair of his favorite jeans, an open-neck chambray shirt and the boots that were usually in the back of the closet. They were old, scuffed, worn at the heels. They were his favorite kick-around boots.

"I...I assumed you were at work," she said, sitting

back to look at him as he neared the table. "You weren't there when I woke up, and I thought you'd left without waking me."

"I wasn't about to wake you up, and I didn't go to work." He held both hands out at his sides. "As you can see. No suit. No briefcase." He tucked the tips of his fingers in the pockets of his jeans and rocked on the balls of his feet toward her. "I'm not going in today or for the next few days."

"Adam, what are you doing?"

He ignored the question and looked at Grace. "Any more of that great coffee?"

Grace motioned to the main kitchen area. "Plenty in there. Help yourself."

"Sounds good." He glanced at Maggie, his expression unreadable, adding to her sense of something coming. "We'll talk in a minute," he said, then turned and went after his coffee.

Maggie looked at Grace, but the older woman was staring out the window. "Douglas isn't going to be a happy camper," Grace murmured, a Texas twang creeping into her soft voice. "Looks like rain's coming."

Douglas, Grace's husband, was as tender as anything with the babies. He'd been there for Adam growing up, when Adam's father had worked to fill the void of losing his wife. "Grace, what's going on?" she asked, the weather not much of a concern to her at the moment. Not when her workaholic husband looked like a ranch hand instead of the corporate lawyer he usually was during the week.

Grace looked at Maggie. "Be patient," she said.

Before Maggie could demand an explanation, Adam was back, but he didn't sit down with the women. He stood by Maggie's chair, sipping his coffee while he squinted out the window. "Looks like rain's coming," he said, echoing Grace's words.

Maggie didn't look out the window. She looked at her husband. She felt bombarded by him, by the clean freshness of soap and denim mingling with the richness of the coffee. He rocked her world when they first met, and he still could. He did. And now, whatever he was up to was adding to that sensation. She felt definitely uneasy. "Adam, I don't care about the weather. Just tell me what's going on. Grace won't, but you'd better. And if it's something to do with the babies, if one of them…" She swallowed hard. "Tell me."

He cast her a narrowed glance that made her heart catch slightly. "Okay, I'll tell you."

Grace stood, taking her coffee. "My cue to go and see if Louise needs help."

"Don't leave," Adam said without looking at her. "You know about this anyway."

"About what?" Maggie asked, looking from Grace to her husband, a degree of panic setting in. "Is it the babies?"

"No, love," Adam said. "No, it's not about them. It's about us."

"Us? What?"

He hesitated, something Adam seldom did, and finally said, "We're making our escape."

"Escape?" Maggie shook her head, her coffee forgotten. "What are you talking about?"

"You and me." He smiled, a slightly unsteady expression that crinkled his eyes and curved his lips. "Three days. Alone. Just the two of us. Grace and Louise will stay with the babies, and—"

She felt relief at the same time she felt shocked at what

he was saying. "Adam, stop. We can't just run away from home. I mean, that's craziness."

His smile faltered, but he came closer and put his coffee on the table next to hers. Dropping to his haunches, he framed her face with his hands. "It's not craziness. It's called survival, and we can. We need to."

"Sure." She exhaled, her insides twisting with nerves. "Of course, I just meant, not now. When we can manage it. It sounds wonderful, just the two of us. But when the babies are older, when they aren't so tiny."

"No, we need to do it now. Grace and Louise will do fine with the babies, and Douglas will be here to help, too. We can go up to the family cabin by the lake. It's open and aired out, just waiting for us to get there."

Maggie covered his hands with hers. "Adam, please, be reasonable. I can't go. I can't just leave."

"Yes, you can," he said in a low voice, no smile on his face now. "You're not irreplaceable, and it's not desertion to leave them for a few days." He drew in a sharp breath. "Maggie, you're not your mother."

She drew back sharply, breaking the contact with him as an ache in her middle almost took her breath away. "That's not fair," she muttered.

"Isn't that what you think? If you leave them at all, you've failed? You've run out on them? You've deserted them? You can't love them and leave them even for a day or two?" He raked his fingers through his hair. "Maggie, listen to me, your mother walked out. She was there one minute, then gone the next. She didn't care and she left. How she could do that to you is unbelievable, but that was her and that isn't you. She left a year-old child without looking back. And she was gone. Do you really think that you're anything like that?"

His words tore at her, bringing back feelings she never

wanted to feel again. "No, of course not." She bit her lip hard, and she closed her eyes tightly to block out his determined expression. "This isn't about my mother. It's about me and my babies. I love them. They're mine."

"I love you, and they're ours."

She sensed him moving. She opened her eyes to find him standing over her, his hands jammed in the pockets of his jeans. "You of all people know what it took to get them here with us. I can't just walk away like that."

"Sweetheart, you can. You can walk out the door with me, know that they're in great hands." His expression narrowed even more. "You couldn't be your mother even if you tried to be."

"I don't want to talk about her." She stood, put some distance between them, then turned and went to the windows to stare at the beginning rain. "She's got nothing to do with this irrational idea of yours."

"Irrational?" he asked from right behind her. "It's irrational that I want to be with you?"

That ache grew, and she hugged her arms around her so tightly that she began to tremble. "That's emotional blackmail," she muttered.

"What?"

"I want to be with you, too, and we'll have time, but right now, it's…it's too soon. Don't force it like this."

"Oh, baby, I'm not doing that. I don't want to do that. That isn't what's going on. I just want you to remember you and me. The two of us."

Her eyes burned and smarted but were painfully dry. "Of course I remember."

"Then what happened to us?"

"It's…we're still here."

"We are…for now," he muttered. "But for how long?"

She turned to Adam and a very silent Grace. "You...
you need to give me time. I thought it would be so easy,
just fall in love, get married and have a baby, then it all
fell apart." She closed her eyes tightly, the images of
months of trying, of treatments and tests, of calling Adam
to come home because "my temperature is just right,"
making love frantically because it had to be then. "But it
worked out, it really did," she said in a shaky voice.
"Five babies. Five lives. And they're so tiny, so fragile.
I thought you wanted them...and loved them as much as
I do, that you'd understand that things could never be the
same again."

He came to her, reaching toward her, and she braced
herself when his hands touched her shoulders. "Good
God, you know I want them and I love them, and I understand how scary this all is. I'm scared, too, and I know
where you're coming from about having to be here all the
time. Your mother walked out on you, just left." She
flinched at his words, but he didn't let go. "And I'm going
to say this one last time. You are not your mother. You're
a loving, caring mother. You almost gave your life for
them." His hands tightened in a spasm, then eased. "I'm
losing you, Maggie, and I can't live if that happens."

Tears were there, hot tears that slipped out of her eyes,
and she began to shake. The next thing she knew, she was
cuddled to Adam's chest, surrounded by the man she
loved, and for an instant, she felt so safe and so complete.
She grabbed at that feeling, but then he spoke again, his
voice a deep rumble against her face pressed to his chest.
"Do you love me?"

"Oh, God, yes," she groaned.

"Then trust me?" He was easing her back but never
letting her go. He studied her with an intensity that made

her world stop. "Let me do this. Let me call the shots. Just three days. You and me?"

She felt as if she were being torn in two. She couldn't let go of Adam or the babies, or those two halves of her life would be permanently separated.

She closed her eyes, barely able to get air in her lungs. There had to be some way to make this right without losing either half of her soul.

Chapter Three

Maggie tried to think of something, anything to make this all better. "What...what if... Maybe we could go away for a day, just the two of us?" she asked.

Adam was silent for what seemed an eternity, never blinking, barely breathing. "A day?" he finally said. "Twenty-four whole hours?"

"Yes, absolutely." Maybe this would work. "We could go next week, when I have everything ready and planned. We could get Grace to come here, and we could maybe go to dinner and a movie, and—"

"No."

The single word stopped her dead. "But why not, Adam?"

"We go now. We have twenty-four hours from now, just you and me. No dinner, no movie, no monitors, no nothing. Just us at the cabin. Right now," he finished in a hoarse voice.

"I...I...don't know if I can," she stammered, wondering how her heart could be so divided between the great loves of her life. It wasn't fair. "I don't know."

"Well, if you don't know, I guess that's it," he said, a flatness touching his voice.

She glanced at Grace, the woman who had been silent through all this, never moving. "Grace?"

"It's your choice," she said evenly.

"But I can't—"

"Oh, you can, you can do it," Grace said.

"But what if something happens? Daniel's been so fussy and Gracie…?"

"I'll be here, sweetheart. I'll be here."

"But I need to be here."

Grace nodded. "Of course you do, and you will be. I can call if there's a problem, and Adam will bring you right back." She came closer to the two of them, her voice growing softer as she spoke. "You need to go, sweetie, you really need to go." The woman looked at Adam, who Maggie knew was as close to a son as Grace had in this world. "And he needs you to go, too."

Maggie looked at Adam. She didn't know if she could do this, but she'd try. She'd really try. She kissed him quickly, needing that grounding, then met his gaze again. "Okay, we'll go. I'll pack and—"

Grace moved closer to the two of them. "You're all packed. Just go up and say goodbye to the little ones, then go and be with your husband."

It felt to Maggie as if she was taking a huge leap off a towering cliff…with no lifeline. Then she felt Adam draw her closer and knew that was wrong. He was her lifeline. She nodded, slipped out of his reach and started across the room. "I'll get dressed," she murmured.

"Casual, nothing fancy," Adam called after her.

She kept going out of the kitchen area and stopped when she was out of sight of her husband and Grace. She hugged her arms tightly around herself to stop a trembling that seemed to be coming from the inside out as Adam's words echoed in her. "You're not your mother."

"I'm not my mother," she muttered to herself as she headed in the direction of the bedrooms. But that didn't stop the horrible feeling that she was abandoning her children. She neared the nursery doors, hesitated and had to force herself not to go inside yet, but to go and get dressed first. Then she'd say goodbye. She'd promise each of them she'd be back in twenty-four hours. She'd keep her promise. She'd be right here in twenty-four hours.

ADAM FELT the tension in Maggie as they drove through the steady rain into the hills. He didn't know if it was wishful thinking on his part or not, but by the time they neared the dirt road that led to the family cabin near the lake, she seemed a bit less anxious.

He believed that until she spoke for the first time in the past hour. "I'm sorry I took so long getting ready, but it seems just too much for Grace to be able to handle all of the babies for a whole day."

"She's up to it. And she's got Louise with her. No problem. But there is a change in plans."

He sensed her dart him a quick look. "What?" she asked, sitting straighter in the seat, turning to him. "What change?"

"Since we didn't get away until later, the twenty-four hours started when we left the house."

"That's it?"

"That's it."

"Okay, twenty-four hours from the time we left the house. It's a deal, as long as you're sure Grace will be okay with them."

"Love, I'd trust her with my life. My dad did, and I trust her with our family."

"And she'll know if the babies need anything, won't she?"

He reached for her hand clenched on her thigh and closed his hand around her fist. "Next to you, she knows those babies better than anyone, even me. And she loves them." He squeezed her hand slightly. "She can tell them apart without looking at the bracelets they wear. She's brilliant."

Thankfully Maggie laughed at that, a weak chuckle, but it was something he relished. "Yes, she is. You still get Julia and Daniel mixed up, and I can't see how you can do that. He's such a boy, and she's so feminine."

Adam chuckled. "Dead right. She looks just like you. Absolutely beautiful."

"And he looks like you, like a real McCallum."

"I don't know if that's good or bad."

"Good, very good," she said, twisting her hand in his until their fingers were laced together.

He pulled her hand to him, kissed it, then drew it down with his to his thigh. "Yes, very good."

He heard her sigh softly in the confines of the black Jeep. "Adam, who would have thought our lives would have gone like this. All that worry and trouble…" She sighed again. "Five babies. What a miracle."

He glanced at her, the love he felt for her beyond words. And his fear when he thought he would lose her as she was having the babies still lingered in the back of his soul. Losing her was beyond anything he could think about. They needed this time alone desperately. "Thanks for coming," he murmured as he turned onto the gravel drive that led up the hill to the cabin and the lake.

She didn't respond, and he darted her a quick look. He was a bit taken aback to see her eyes closed tightly. Then they crested the hill in the road, which ended in the drive-way to the sprawling cabin. The log and shingle structure his father had helped build the year before he was born was ahead of them, the steady rain robbing the afternoon of light and making the building look a bit foreboding.

He drove under the protection of a jutting portico that shadowed the stairs that led to a wraparound porch and massive carved doors. He stopped the car and turned to Maggie, letting his gaze skim over her. She was achingly lovely even in an oversize gray sweatshirt, slender jeans and chunky boots.

She'd taken him at his word. Nothing fancy. Not even any makeup. Her short, feathery cap of hair framed her delicately boned face, a thinner face since the babies had come. And those eyes that had shadows they shouldn't have and looked tired too much lately. She wouldn't take the offer of more help, almost frantic to be with each baby as much as she could be.

She looked at him, a fleeting glance from under lashes that needed no mascara to enhance them. "I almost forgot about this place. It's been so long."

This was the place they had first made love, and the place, he was certain now, the babies had been conceived. Their place. No one else in the family came out here anymore. Not even his father. It had become theirs until the babies were on the way. Then it had been shuffled to one side, the way so many things had been in the past months. But now they were here, together, and the magic was still here for him.

He let go of her hand to lightly brush her cheek with the back of his fingers, deep shadows cast there by the soft green of the dash lights. Her body heat radiated into him. "Damn straight it's been too long," he murmured roughly, and leaned toward her, tasting her soft lips before pulling back. If he could have smiled then, he would have, but he felt unsteady, and his need for her was unbearable. "Do you remember the first time we came here?"

He felt her tremble slightly, and she said, "How could I forget? I hadn't ever been out of the city, and here I was in the middle of the wilderness."

"The wilderness? It's a lake and some trees, not the end of civilization." He smiled, an easy expression to muster as he remembered her thinking she could hike in suede boots or that he could be here alone with her and not want to make love to her. "Although I seem to remember that you thought it was when we couldn't get pizza delivered and you were shocked that we used real wood in the fireplace and didn't have gas logs."

Her soft chuckle sounded delicious to him. "The roles were changed, weren't they? Me, the teacher, and you were teaching me about roughing it."

He remembered just what they taught each other that first time, and his body began to ache in the most wonderful way. "You taught me a lot, too." He slipped his hand behind her neck, burying his fingers in the silky fringe of hair. "You taught me that two people can meet, a simple meeting, looking at each other, and that it could change my life. I fell madly in love with you." He grinned at her. "We taught each other so much, and the second time we came here, we knew exactly what to do, didn't we?"

"Exactly," she whispered and leaned toward him, her lips a feathery caress on his, then her breath brushing his skin with warmth. "I can't believe that we found each other like that," she said in a low, unsteady voice. Then he felt her tremble. "Can we go inside?"

She didn't have to ask him more than once. He moved away from her, got out of the Jeep and strode through the cold damp air to go around to her door. She opened it, and before she could get out, he reached for her, taking her hand again. "Come on," he said, taking her with him up the two steps that led to the wraparound porch.

She took two steps at once to keep up with him. He let her go long enough to get the key out of his pocket, unlock the door and swing it open. Then he turned to her. The ancient trees that framed the front of the cabin, the way the rain blurred the day around them, were lost on him. All he saw was Maggie. "Twenty-four hours," he murmured. "I'm not wasting any of it."

She grinned, a fantastic expression that hit deep in his being, then she was moving past him into the cabin, breathing, "Amen." He moved with her, thankful Grace had taken care of everything so quickly. The cabin seemed as if it was waiting for them, aired and ready. Maggie flipped on the overhead light and turned to him, inches separating them. "Okay, we're here, and I'm open to anything," she said, a slight huskiness in her voice. "So, swimming is doable in the rain. Hiking? Nah," she said with a shake of her head. "Fishing is questionable."

He swung the door shut before he went closer to her, sensing her heat but not touching her…yet. It was just like old times. The slight smile. The teasing. That connection, and for a moment, he couldn't remember why he'd been afraid for them. "Can I add to your list of possible activities?"

"You can do anything you want."

He touched her then, lightly cupping her chin with one hand. "Anything? Are you sure?"

She pressed her hands flat against his chest, and he knew that his heart was hammering. "I trust you, and I'm very sure," she whispered. His breath caught when her hands slowly moved lower and her hand found the fastener at the waist of his jeans. She tugged at it, unsnapping it. "I'm very sure."

As she said those words, all the things that had made these twenty-four hours happen were more than worth it. Missed business meetings, a deposition that wouldn't happen on time, paying Louise double to stay with Grace and Douglas, getting past the fact that his father had seen what was happening to them so clearly.

"Okay, you've got it. We're going back to the beginning, to when it all started," he said as he swept her into his arms. He stopped just long enough to kiss her fiercely before carrying her into the bedroom at the back of the cabin, into shadows and the sound of rain beating on the French doors that lined the back of the room.

Maggie had never lived in the past. The present and the future fascinated and intrigued her and were full enough to keep her more than busy. But for that split second, she *was* back at the beginning, to the first time Adam had picked her up like this in the cabin. To that moment when she knew that she would give herself to him because she loved him, and knew that her life was never going to be the same because of him.

She held him, her eyes closed tightly as she tried to absorb the overwhelming feelings that flooded through her. Love and completeness. Everything she'd wanted all her life, everything she'd found in this man from the start, everything she'd forgotten in the middle of the business of their new lives. They moved together, his voice a rumble against her cheek where it rested in the hollow of his shoulder. "I love you," he said, his voice as unsteady as she felt.

Then he was easing her down into the coolness of the linen, and she opened her eyes to the main bedroom in the cabin, to the vaulted wooden ceilings, whitewashed walls and the sound of rain against the windows that overlooked the view of the water. Adam was with her in the bed, gathering her to him, and in that moment, nothing else existed.

A crack of thunder made her jump slightly, then a flash of lightning washed the room in brilliance, moving over Adam so close to her. It exposed the lines etched in his face, the plane of his strong jaw, eyes filled with a fire that echoed in her. She reached to touch him, feeling the prickling of a new beard at his chin, then her forefinger touched his lips, so soft, such a contradiction to the hardness of the man.

He took her finger into his mouth, into heat and warmth, and the seductive act made her tremble. Love was such an inadequate word for what she felt for him, and loneliness was such an inadequate word for what she felt when he wasn't there.

He shifted, his hand slipping under her sweatshirt, and his eyes never left hers. A smile came when his hand skimmed on her bare skin, finding no bra, just the weight of her full breasts. His smile was crooked, his chuckle rough. ''You really didn't dress up, did you?'' he murmured.

''Well, we were short on time, and I didn't want to waste any of it with any...'' Her voice stopped on a shudder when he bent toward her and touched his lips to her throat, finding a spot by her ear that sent signals deep into her being. Then the shirt was being slipped off, and the jeans followed. Adam's hands against her naked skin, his heat mingling with hers and the beating of the rain on the windows only echoed her heartbeat.

There was an urgency in her, a fierce need for him that shook her. It had only started the other night. She tugged at his clothes, needing to feel him, to know him, to be part of him. Then his clothes were gone, tossed away, and she and Adam lay together, their bodies entwined in the cool linen, her head against his heart, his breath ruffling her hair as the storm built outside.

"I want this to last forever." He breathed roughly as his hands slipped lower, skimming over the curve of her hip, then circling to the front, splaying his fingers on her stomach. "For it to never stop."

She felt a slight hesitation as his hand explored her, the way her body had changed after the babies still bothering her a bit. Adam stopped, his hand still on her abdomen, and he drew back to look at her. "What?"

She felt foolish and vain, but she told him the truth. "I wish..." She bit her lip, startled at the tears that burned behind her eyes. "Oh, shoot," she muttered, falling back to stare at the ceiling. "I wish I worked out ten hours a day and jogged every morning."

"You do a lot more just taking care of the babies," he said, so close to her that his breath played warmly across her bare breasts.

She was shocked that she hadn't thought of the babies for a while. She'd forgotten to remember, and that brought her up short. "Do you think I should call Grace?" she asked as she twisted toward him, their legs tangling together.

"No." The single word came out abruptly, then he softened it. "It's only been a few hours, and she's got the number here."

"I know, I know, but what if—"

He touched her lips with two fingers, hushing her completely. "Maggie, love, stop it. Twenty-four hours. The two of us. Remember?"

"I remember," she said, trying to focus, to regain that feeling from just moments ago.

"I thought you said I could do anything I wanted to do," he whispered, and moved, startling her when his lips found her nipple. It peaked immediately, and she groaned spontaneously, her thoughts jumbling from the pure pleasure of his touch on her. ''I want to do this,'' he murmured against her skin, and his hand slipped lower, tracing the curve of her hip. ''And this.'' He touched her stomach again, then slipped lower. ''And definitely this.'' He breathed hoarsely as he found her center.

He pressed his hand against her, moving slowly, and she arched against his touch without even thinking about what she was doing. Every thought was gone. She wanted him. She needed him. Then his fingers slipped into her, and she gasped, lifting her hips to meet his hand. She felt him deep inside her, then he was gone, and in the next instant, he was over her, and she felt him against her again. His hard strength touched her, tested her with its velvety heat. Then, as she wrapped her legs around his hips, he pressed into her, deeply and completely into her.

Both of them were motionless for a long moment, savoring the sensation, the oneness, then Adam was moving, slowly at first, then faster, a pace that matched her aching need for him. She met him, over and over again, feeling that building of ecstasy that threatened to shatter her into a million pieces. Until the apex came. The final thrust, that instant when there was nothing between the two of them, when for a split second in eternity, she melted right into Adam and became one with him.

She heard a voice cry out and knew that it was hers, the pleasure beyond anything she could absorb, the climax together, pure sensation and release. Then she was with Adam, tangled with him, holding him, the rain beating outside and his heart beating against her cheek. The babies had been conceived on a night like this, that one time in all those months when their lovemaking had been intense and spontaneous, without any mention of the thermometer or it being "the right time." They'd come to relax, and they'd ended up making the babies.

She snuggled closer to Adam, holding him, loving him for being a part of the five tiny lives. But even as she rested with him, she had to fight the urge to call home and check on those lives. So tiny, so fragile. She felt his breathing start to even out, and she made herself lie there. She made herself close her eyes, and she made herself try to not think about anything but the moment.

But no matter how hard she tried, she couldn't sleep, and she couldn't get past the niggling feeling that something could be wrong, that the babies might need her. She felt Adam's heart against her cheek, felt him take one easy breath after the other. He was sleeping, and all she could think of was being so far from the babies.

Grace would call her, she told herself. She'd promised. Then thunder tore through the cabin, followed by the brilliance of lightning flooding the bedroom. What if the phones were out? The cell phone was in the car. Maybe the cabin phone hadn't even been hooked up. She should have checked. She should have made sure.

She waited as long as she could, then eased back from Adam. She'd just check. And if the phone didn't work, she could get the cell phone. Adam would never have to know. He'd sleep, and she'd be back before he woke and knew anything about it. She'd just make sure.

Chapter Four

Adam woke to soft darkness, rain beating against the cabin windows and an empty bed beside him. He shifted, felt coolness in the sheets, then opened his eyes and pushed himself to a sitting position. "Maggie?" he called through the shadows as he looked around. The room was empty, and it was night. The rain was really coming down, and a damp chill was in the air.

"Maggie?" he called again. Nothing.

He got up, and without bothering with any clothes, crossed to open the bathroom door, but Maggie wasn't there. He turned, listening, but couldn't hear anything. He went to the bedroom door, opened it but only found shadows, chilly air and the echoing sound of rain beating on the windows. No Maggie.

"Maggie?"

Nothing.

For a moment Adam had the real fear that Maggie had gone, that she'd driven off back to the house. The he saw that the front door was ajar. As he started for it, he heard footsteps on the porch, then the door was pushed open and Maggie was there.

With the stormy night at her back, she looked almost

waiflike in the gray sweatshirt, bare legs and feet, her eyes deeply shadowed. "Where in the hell?"

She held up the cell phone. "The house phone is out, and I went out to the car to get the cell," she said, coming in and closing the door.

"Why?"

"I told you, the house phone isn't working."

She came closer, and he could see the way she was holding the phone, as if it were her lifeline. "What's going on?"

"I just…" She bit her lip and was so close that he could catch the scent of her in the air. "Adam, I was going to call Grace," she said, then added quickly, "just to check."

She tilted her head, watching him, trying to read him, and all he could think of was he sort of liked her short hair now. It exposed the sweep of her neck when she tilted her head that way, an enticing invitation.

"I need to check, Adam," she said when he didn't respond. "You can understand that, can't you?"

Of course he could, and he did. "Just what do you think's going on?"

"That's just it, I don't know." She shrugged, a painfully vulnerable action of her slender shoulders. "I'm going to call," she said, but didn't move to put in the number. She watched him with a touch of uncertainty.

Did she think he'd forbid her to call? Had he come across as that heartless? That pained him. "Go ahead and call," he said, then added, "then we can get back into bed."

He'd meant to be suggestive, to retrieve a trace of that passion that had been there between them so recently, but that didn't happen. Before he'd finished his statement, she was dialing the number to home on the cell phone and pressing the send button.

"Grace, it's Maggie. I just…" She glanced at Adam. "I wanted to make sure everything is okay."

As he watched her, he saw the uncertainty change. Her eyes widened slightly, and her mouth tightened. "What?" she asked with a touch of tension in her voice.

He went closer, catching her eyes, motioning to the phone. "What's going on?" he whispered, but she barely looked at him.

"Exactly what did he say?" she asked.

She listened intently, and when Adam laid his hands on her shoulders from behind, he felt her jerk with shock. She twisted, looked at him, then spoke into the phone again. "I knew it. I shouldn't have…" He felt her release a shuddering breath. "I'll be there as soon as I can." She closed her eyes tightly as she listened for a brief moment before saying, "I said I'll be there."

She hit the end button, dropped the phone on a chair then slipped out of Adam's touch and headed to the bedroom. "What's going on?" he asked, going after her.

She didn't stop, but spoke over her shoulder. "Jackson's sick. He's got a fever and…" Her voice was lost when she disappeared into the other room.

He ran, getting into the room to find her putting on her jeans. "Sick?" he asked, his heart hurting from the shock and fear of thinking that one of the babies was sick, that he'd forced this outing on Maggie and this had happened. "What's wrong?"

She pushed her legs into her jeans, zipped the zipper and started looking frantically around the room. "My shoes, where are they?" she asked, and dropped to her knees to look under the huge poster bed.

"Maggie, stop and tell me what's going on."

"I told you, Jackson's sick. I have to get back there."

She stood with her boots in her hands, then sat on the edge of the bed to put them on. Adam grabbed his jeans and put them on, then turned to a frantic Maggie who could barely push her feet into her boots. He crossed to her and dropped to his haunches in front of her. "Stop and explain this to me. How sick is he? What is it? What did the doctor say?"

She kept lacing her boots, not looking at him at all. "Sick. He's got a fever and he's flushed and he's crying." She stopped and looked at him. "I could hear him crying," she whispered. "I need to get back to him."

She tried to stand, but Adam stopped her by pressing his hands on her shoulders, holding her down. "What did the doctor say?" he said, trying to keep calm.

"Grace put in a call for him." She tried to get free of his hold. "We can't waste any time. We'll talk in the car."

"No, you sit still and take a deep breath. I'll call Grace and then we'll figure out what to do."

She twisted to free herself. "Adam, what's to figure out? Jackson's sick, and we can't waste any time."

She slipped past him so quickly that he barely had time to move out of her way to keep from being pushed backward. He got to his feet and followed her into the great room, almost running into her back when she stopped abruptly and turned to him. "Where's my purse?"

"In the car," he muttered, before saying, "Let me call Grace," as he picked up the phone.

"Call anyone you want to call," she said, her face slightly flushed. "But do it while we drive, okay?"

He motioned to the windows and the rain. "It's pouring out there. If we don't need to go, let's not do it."

"What?" she gasped, looking as shocked as if he'd said that he was an alien. "Not do it? Just not go?"

He held up one hand, palm out. "I didn't say that, but give me one minute before we go running out into that storm. Just give me one minute?"

"He's sick, Adam, and he's so tiny, and I'm not there. I don't know why you're arguing with me."

"You think I'm not scared about this? God, after everything we went through to have the babies. I'm scared spitless, but I want to figure it out. I want to—"

"Do whatever you want, but I'm going," she said and turned from him, half running toward the entry.

He went after her, catching up as she opened the front door and a blast of cold, damp air burst into the cabin. She headed for the car, stopped by the passenger door and turned to him. "Are you going to come?"

"Maggie, look around you," he said, pointing to the stormy night. "It would take hours to get back to the house, *if* we could even get through. The roads are going to be a mess, and you know how the roads get in heavy rain this time of year."

He might just as well have been talking to the wall for all the good his logic did. Maggie pulled the door open, climbed in the passenger seat, then turned to him. "Are you coming?"

He held up the phone. "One call."

She closed her eyes, scrunching them tightly, the way a child would who was angry or upset. "Okay, okay," she muttered. "Just do it, then you'll see, and we can get going."

He quickly dialed home. The phone rang once, then Grace answered and he heard the sound of crying in the background.

"Grace? It's Adam. What's going on?"

"Adam. Thank goodness you called. I didn't mean to upset Maggie, but she asked, and I told her that Jackson's fussy and got a bit of a fever. Nothing big. The doctor thinks it's probably just teething, told me what to do, and he'll be on call if things get worse.''

He felt a partial easing in his chest. ''You think that's it, just teething?''

''I'd bet it is. The doctor seemed pretty certain.'' The crying was almost drowning her out. ''He's not a happy camper, but he's got great lungs.''

''Maggie's pretty upset,'' he said, a real understatement. He watched her in the car. Hands clenched in her lap, her eyes shut, her head and shoulders shaking slightly from tension. ''I just wanted to check and make sure we didn't need to head back.''

''Oh, honey, no, don't do that. Babies get sick. It's part of the growing process. And you and Maggie need to be there. You need time. Your dad's worried, and so am I. Just stay put, and I promise I'll call if anything changes.''

''Okay,'' he said, feeling a huge weight lifting off him as Grace spoke. ''Call if there's any change, otherwise, we'll be back around noon tomorrow. Okay?''

''You got it,'' Grace said, then hung up.

Adam looked at Maggie in the car. ''Get out and come inside. Grace says that things are okay.''

She turned to him. ''What?''

''Jackson's got a fever, and he's probably teething, and that's not life and death.''

She didn't move. ''How does she know that?''

''That's what the doctor said.''

''The doctor saw him?''

''No, but he called and they discussed it, and that's what he thinks is going on.''

''A phone conference? That doesn't mean anything. It's a guess.''

''An educated guess.''

She leaned toward him earnestly. "It's a guess, and if I were there, I could tell. I know my babies. I really know them. A mother's supposed to, and I do."

"Maggie, stop it."

"Adam, it could be serious. You know how careful we had to be when they first came home. How…how delicate they were, and they still are. We can't just let it go."

"Of course we can't. But Grace will be with him, and if things change, she'll call." He held out his hand to her. "Come back inside with me, please?"

She looked at his hand, almost recoiling from it. "We have to go home."

"No, we don't. We've got our time here, and Grace is—"

"She's not his mother, Adam," she almost yelled at him. "We have to go back." She gulped in air. "I have to go back."

He had thought getting her here would be a turning point, that time together would make her realize what they had was precious and fleeting and that they could balance their life with the kids. But in that moment he knew that was all a dream, his dream. He loved her and always would, but he didn't have her. Not even after being so close to her physically. He didn't have her, and he desperately wanted to have her and hold her forever. He drew back his hand and felt as if he'd lost the biggest gamble of his life.

"No, *we* don't," he murmured.

Thunder and lightning cracked around them, and the light was colorless and dead as she said, "I'm going to our child. Are you coming with me?"

He stood very still, looking at her and aching for what wasn't there anymore, blotted out by her obsession. "No. And I want you to stay here with me."

"Adam, don't, please, don't."

"Don't what? I want you with me. I want you here, and there's no real emergency, and it's storming out here."

She bit her lip hard. "I can't be that selfish."

"Selfish? Selfish? What in the hell are you talking about?" He was almost yelling. "You think I'm being selfish, being reasonable?"

"I don't know, but I know that I can't think of myself...or of you. Not when Jackson is so sick. That's not what a mother does. That isn't what a mother should do."

He understood. He didn't doubt her great love for her children. She'd almost died to get them into the world. But this went way beyond that and in an entirely different direction. "That's it, isn't it? It's always the same. She walked out and left you. She turned her back and was never there for you, not when you were sick or well. So you're going to be there, even if it's just for sniffles? Even if Grace can do anything you can do? Even if we've spent most of the last year never taking any time for ourselves?"

"We came here," she murmured shakily. "We've had time together. And it was terrific, but now we can't just say, 'forget everything,' and do whatever we want and damn the cost."

"We aren't. We..." He went closer and touched her cheek, barely making contact with the tip of his forefinger on her cold skin, not trusting himself to make the touch any more substantial. "We are the core of this family, you and me, and if we don't make this work, there is no core." He drew back. "There is no family."

"Oh, Adam, that's not so. We've got time. The babies aren't going to be like this forever. They'll grow up and be wonderful people, but we have to be there for them."

"We are, and we have been and we always will be, but what about their mother and father?"

She shrugged, an oddly fluttery movement of her shoulders. "We're here. And we're okay."

"Are we?"

"Adam, please, this is a waste of time, we need—"

"Maggie, we aren't okay, and we haven't been for a long time. Dad knew, and Grace and Douglas."

"You've been talking to them about us?"

"No, they talked to me."

She took a harsh breath, then moved into the shadows of the car. "Are you coming with me?"

He stood back. "No, I'm not."

She hesitated, then shifted to the driver's seat and fumbled to get her key out of her purse and into the ignition. "I'm sorry about tonight," she said as the car roared to life. "We'll have time later, when the babies are okay."

"Don't count on it," he said, grabbing the open door and leaning in toward her. "All we've got is right now."

"That's ridiculous, and I don't have time to argue with you now. I'm going home to Jackson. Are you coming?"

"Dammit, Maggie, be reasonable."

"I'm not being unreasonable," she muttered, then said, "you are."

"That's it?"

"What more is there?"

He stared at her hard, etching her image into his mind. "Nothing, I guess," he said and swung the door shut.

Whatever emptiness he'd felt lately was nothing compared to what he felt at that moment. The void in his soul threatened to consume him. The tires of the Jeep squealed as Maggie drove off into the storm and the night, and all he could do was watch her go. It wasn't supposed to be like this. It wasn't supposed to hurt to love her. It wasn't supposed to be so damn hard to talk to her. And it wasn't supposed to end.

He watched the glow of the taillights heading down the dirt drive, the rain smearing the dark hulk of the car as it went farther and farther away. "Dammit, dammit, dammit," he muttered. He was a man who was used to being able to make anything work, and he felt useless and empty. "Dammit!" he screamed into the night, and at the same moment, the lights of the car veered to the left, but the driveway went right at that point. It curved right under the trees, then out to the highway. But the lights went left, left where the bank dropped in a ravine, a twenty-foot drop. Then the lights disappeared, and all there was was darkness.

"Maggie!" he screamed as he took off running into the rain.

MAGGIE DROVE AWAY from Adam, the ache in her deep and piercing. But she couldn't turn back. She had to be there for Jackson, and for the others. Adam couldn't ask her to turn her back on the babies. He couldn't. And she wouldn't.

She drove as quickly as she could onto the dirt drive that was mud, and she felt the Jeep slip slightly to the right, then it was on course and heading for the main road. The rain beat all around her, blurring the windshield and making the glow from the headlights a watery smear in front of her.

She saw the trees at the curve and jerked the wheel too hard to the right. Perversely, the car didn't go to the right. She felt it lose traction and slide slightly to the left, almost of its own will, and she yanked the steering wheel to the right while she almost stood on the brakes. But that only made it worse, and she knew, in that second, that she wasn't in control. She wasn't in control of anything, not where the Jeep was going or her life.

The car swung hard to the right, toward the trees, then the trees disappeared and she saw nothing but blackness coming for her. She couldn't be flying, that was impossible, but there was the oddest feeling of floating, then a hard, jarring impact that drove the air out of her lungs, then another and another.

She tried to hold on to the steering wheel, but it was yanked out of her hands, and all she could think about was Adam and the children, of him saying that all they had was now. And she had nothing. The world tipped to one side, and she braced herself for a full flip, but it didn't come. She was slammed against the door despite the seat belt, then back again.

She braced herself for a horrendous impact, for the end of this and maybe everything. And grief filled her soul. Regret and horror in equal measure. She wouldn't be there for the babies, the one thing she'd feared most for them. And she wouldn't be there for Adam. The thing she feared most for herself.

Then, miraculously, everything stopped for a long moment, then there was a groan, a shudder, and the car went nose first, straight down, and with a hard thud, it stopped, almost vertical.

"Thank you, thank you, thank you," she breathed over and over again as she gripped the steering wheel, pressing her head against the cold plastic. She tried to feel her body beyond the hammer of her heart and the gulping of air into her lungs. She waited for pain, but there was no real pain. A dull ache in the side of her head, tightness in her chest and side, and pressure on her legs. But no agony, except in her heart.

Chapter Five

The car wasn't moving. Maggie knew the ravine was at least twenty feet deep. She had no idea how far she'd gone down, but the angle of the car was ominous. As ominous as the motor stalling and the dash lights flickering and rain soaking her from the back. She couldn't see outside, not with mud, leaves and rain streaking the windows, but she knew one thing for certain. She was alive, and she had to get out of the car before it plunged and flipped.

In the dim green glow from the dash lights she could see the air bag laying on her like a deflated silver balloon, hanging to where the leather covering in the center of the steering wheel had ripped in four directions. She hadn't heard or seen it inflate, but it was there. She pushed it off her chest, then with fingers that barely cooperated, she managed to loosen the seat belt, and the pressure on her chest and side eased.

There was a chemical smell in the air mingling with the rain and earth. Then she caught a hint of gasoline and panicked all over again. Frantically she tugged the belt off and reached for the door handle, pulling on it with all her might, but nothing happened. It felt almost loose, and the door wasn't giving at all. She twisted to pull the lock button up, but it was jammed at a funny angle in the leather panel, and the button for the window made a whining sound but didn't move the window down.

She twisted, trying to pull her legs away from the pressure against them, and saw where the rain came from, and realized it was her way out. The back window had shattered, letting in the driving rain but giving her an escape hatch. She tried to tug her legs up and across the console, and that was when she felt some pain. Something ran across her shins, and she twisted, pulling, felt a scraping on them, then her feet were free. Twisting, she grabbed at the back of the seat, pulled on the wet leather and managed to ease herself into the gap between the two front seats. She tumbled onto the soaked back seat, then grabbed and finally got a hold on the lower edge of the broken window.

Rain streamed in, running cold over her everywhere, and the edge of the window scraped her skin. She tugged the sleeve of her sweatshirt over her right hand and used the fabric as a barrier, then pulled on the window ledge to get out.

"Maggie!" Adam's voice was there, coming out of the darkness, through the wind and rain that was invading the car. Echoing through her. Then it came again, closer and more real. "Maggie! Maggie!"

"Adam?" she called hoarsely, pushing with her feet, scrambling into the window frame, trying to avoid the broken glass that was everywhere. She levered herself with her elbow against the side and pushed with all her strength, breaking into the night and the storm. She was partway out and pushed with her feet on the back seat, then almost tumbled onto the back door of the Jeep. She barely got her legs free, then she felt her whole body sliding on the slick metal. Flailing for something to stop her fall, she found nothing until someone found her.

Strong hands grabbed her right arm, stopping her slide, twisting her to the edge of the door. Then she was being gathered. She was safe. Even with the storm beating around her, the rain drenching her, she was with Adam, and everything was right. She held him, her face pressed to his bare chest soaked by the rain, and he was speaking, his voice rumbling through her. "Maggie, Maggie, Maggie," he whispered over and over again, and she could feel him shaking. Maybe it was her shaking, too, but she couldn't tell. She just held him for dear life.

He was here. Here and now. And she was alive. That's all that mattered. "Oh, Adam," she breathed, the shaking in her body growing at an alarming rate.

"Are you okay?" he asked, trying to hold her to look at her, but she held on tightly, fighting any gap in their contact.

"I...I...thought..." She gasped against his bare chest. "I thought...I really thought..." She bit her lip hard and tasted the metallic sharpness of blood. "I'm okay," she finished on a shudder.

"Thank God," he murmured, his arms around her tightening to hover just this side of real pain with their pressure. "Thank God."

Then she realized that all he had on was his jeans, and the rain was cold and driving. The wind felt bitter through her wet clothes. "We...we need to get you inside," she said, drawing away but holding his arms as she looked at him in the night and the storm. His hair was plastered to his head, and she looked at his feet, all but buried in the muddy bank by the ruined car, then at him.

"You...you're barefoot," she said.

"And you're alive," he breathed, leaning down to kiss her, heat and comfort in that contact, and it lingered despite the pounding elements around them. Then he drew back. "Let's get up to the house now."

She looked beyond him and saw then just how far into the ravine she'd plunged. The dark shadows of brush and weeds climbed above them, and there was a huge swath of damage caused by the Jeep. "How?" she asked.

"We can do it." It was all he said as he grabbed her hand and turned, reaching with his free hand for the heavy brush to his right. "Just follow me. Think about dry and warm and a hot shower."

She went with him, but all she could think of was him, and him saying that you never knew how much time you had. That you couldn't count on tomorrow and today was all there was. And the babies, how tiny and needy they were, and how much they needed both her and Adam. It seemed to take forever, but they finally climbed onto the drive, and Adam turned to her, lifting her off her feet in one motion.

"You don't have to—"

"Oh, yes, I do," he muttered and carried her up the drive toward the cabin.

Neither of them spoke until they were inside and Adam was lowering her to stand in front of him in the great room. The lights were off, but she didn't need light to see her husband, to see everything about him. And everything about herself. "Adam, I—"

He leaned toward her, touching her lips with his fingers, a cold contact that made her shiver. "Shh, you need a hot shower. You need dry clothes. Then we'll talk. I promise."

He was right. She needed time to think, to sort through things. She shivered again and admitted, "You're right."

"Okay, go and get your shower." He drew back, not touching her anymore, and she was unable to read his expression. That bothered her more than the mud, the rain and the scrapes that were stinging.

"I'll...I won't be long," she murmured and hurried into the master bedroom.

Adam watched her go, then went in the opposite direction, to the kitchen, then to the room off the laundry. There was a small shower there that they used after swimming, and he stripped off his jeans, turned on the water and stepped under it.

He wished he could push that image of the Jeep disappearing out of his mind. But he couldn't, any more than he could get rid of that moment of pure, raw panic and fear that had gripped him. Running through the storm, rocks pressing on his bare feet, slipping and sliding down the ravine to the ominously still car—the events were etched in his mind.

He thought she was dead, that he was right where his father had been so many years before. Alone. With children he adored but the love of his life gone. And it was almost too much to bear. Until he'd seen her crawling out of the car window, sliding down the slick metal. Then she had been in his arms. Real and alive. Holding him. His life.

He scrubbed at his cold skin, trying to get warm, trying to focus on here and now. On Maggie and on him. And he knew what he had to do. He got out, turned off the water and grabbed a towel. He dried himself, then wrapped the towel around his hips and headed through the house. He knew what he had to do, and he knew he should have done it sooner. He should have known that it was the only thing he could do.

MAGGIE STEPPED OUT of the shower, wrapped herself in her white terry-cloth robe and stood very still in the steamy bathroom. Focus, focus. That's what she had to do. She had to stop these scattered fears and dreads. She had to get to what Adam had said, the core of them. The connection they had, that she prayed they still had.

She flipped off the light and stepped into the master bedroom, and Adam was there. His hair was slicked back from his face, exposing a tightness in his expression that was almost painful to see. She dropped her gaze and saw the towel riding low on his lean hips, the dark hair just above it. The flat stomach. Her mouth went suddenly dry, and words that seemed to be bombarding her deep inside wouldn't come out.

He was very still, then he came across to her, looking at her, studying her with narrowed eyes. She realized he had something in his hand, and he was holding it out to her. The cell phone. She looked at it, not touching it.

"Call Grace," he said. "Don't tell her about the accident, but tell her that we'll both be there as soon as we can make it."

She looked at him, not understanding. "Adam, the car's ruined. It's my fault, and now we're stuck, and—"

"Please, just call her. I'll work out the details."

"No," she said, putting her hands behind her back.

"What are you talking about? No? You couldn't wait to get back home, and now you're not even going to call Grace?"

It sounded insane, but suddenly she knew exactly what she had to do. "Grace…she's with Jackson, and she…she can call," Maggie said, her throat getting tighter with each word. "Adam, I'm so sorry."

He was very still, then he said in a voice so low she almost couldn't make out the words, "You're sorry for what?"

She turned from him, hoping that if she wasn't facing him, she could get this out. It had to said. "For doing that. For crashing the car. For putting you through all this. For acting so…so irresponsibly."

"Maggie, don't do this," he said from close behind her, but she didn't turn. Instead she went toward the French doors and stared out at the storm.

"No, I need to say this while I can still get it out," she said with raw frankness. "You were right about me. My mother…she…she walked out. She just left."

He touched her then, his hands on her shoulders, and she closed her eyes tightly. "You don't have to—"

"I do," she said, shrugging to stop his touch. She couldn't do this if he was touching her. "I never really told you what happened. About my mother. She walked out, she left. But she didn't just disappear one day. She left a note, and my dad, until he died, carried it with him. I only found it after he was gone. It was just before I met you."

"You never said anything," he murmured.

"I didn't think I should. I mean, it was so personal, and it was so sad. She left because she couldn't deal with anything. She left because she was so overwhelmed with her life that the best thing she could think to do was not be there. I wasn't even a year old, and she told Dad to take care of me because she couldn't. She wasn't meant to be a mother, and she knew it."

The words seemed flat to her ears, almost devoid of

emotion, yet it was ripping her heart out to tell Adam what she should have told him from the start. "So she just left me there. She never said she loved me. She never said she'd miss me. She just left."

"Oh, God," he whispered and he touched her, putting his arms around her and pulling her against him. And she stayed there, her eyes closed, the note written on a torn scrap of paper so vivid in front of her that she could have been looking at it right then. "I'm so sorry."

"You were right. I almost thought that I could be like that... I'm not like her. I'm not. And when I met you, I loved you so fiercely, I knew I could love. And then the babies, my God, five of them, and so tiny and wonderful, and I loved them with all my heart."

She felt his chin rest on top of her head, and he held her more tightly. "I've told you and told you that you aren't your mother. Now I know you aren't."

"But what if I got overwhelmed, what if I couldn't take it anymore, what if—"

"You are overwhelmed and you can't take it anymore, but your first instinct was to go right back to the babies, to be there, to dive right in and love them. Don't you see, you've been where she was, and you came out of it still here, still loving them, still wanting to be with them above anything or anyone else." He pressed a kiss to her hair. "Maggie, you went through fire, and all you've worried about is them getting burned. You won. You're here."

His words sank into her soul, and she felt a peace she hadn't felt since seeing that note. She felt whole and she felt right. And it was Adam who gave that to her. Who showed her that truth. And she loved him with a love that was staggering. She twisted in his hold, facing him, pressing her body as close to his as was humanly possible.

Loving him more than she loved life itself. Tears were there, sliding down her cheeks, but there was no misery in her, just thanksgiving. "Adam, I realize what I have to do now," she whispered.

He gazed at her. "I know. I'll find a car, some way to get you home."

"No, that's not what I meant," she said, resting her hands on his bare chest, feeling his heart, wondering how his heart could feel so much like hers.

"What do you mean?"

"I want to call home. I need to. You understand that, don't you?"

"I told you I do."

"But what you don't understand is, it's okay not to go if Grace says she's got things under control. It's okay to stay here, you and me."

"Maggie, you can go if I can find a car. Maybe I'll call Dad or have some neighbor come over, but you'll go."

"Give me the phone," she said, moving away from him and holding out her hand. "Just give it to me."

He stared at her for a long moment, then turned, reached for the phone he'd dropped on a chair nearby, then handed it to her. "Here."

She put in their home number, then pressed Send and looked at him. She never looked away as she heard the ringing. Then Grace answered.

"Grace, it's Maggie."

"Oh, sweetie, I'm so glad you called."

That lurch of her heart was there, that fear in her that something had happened, but she wasn't doing this alone. She reached for Adam, took his hand in her free hand, then spoke into the receiver. "What is it?"

"Jackson, he's okay. No fever, still fussy, but he's actually sleeping now. I'm so glad Adam talked you out of coming back. There's no need for that.''

"Grace, Adam's right here. Tell him what you told me, okay?''

"Sure, sweetie, you two have a good time, and I'll see you tomorrow.''

Maggie held the phone out to Adam, and when she saw him hesitate, she said, "It's okay," and the relief in his expression was overwhelming. "Jackson's okay.''

He closed his eyes for a moment, then took the phone and said, "Grace?''

He was silent. Maggie watched him, and his eyes never left hers. "Thanks, yes, we will," he said, then hung up.

He tossed the phone on the chair, then came toward Maggie. "I'll still make it happen if you want to go back.''

She looked at him. "Do you know how much I love you?''

He exhaled in a rush. "I know how much you love the babies, too.''

"Adam, you were so right—if there's no you and me, there's no family. You and me. We're the start and the finish, and the babies are the middle part. I started this with you, and I'll be here at the end, but in the between times I still want you here. I want us here. Do you understand? I'm not leaving. I can't. I won't.''

He came to her without a word, gathering her to him, and they stood for what seemed forever, just holding each other. Each relishing the presence of the other, the reality that they were here, that they'd made it this far. And she was bound and determined that they'd make it to the end. She wasn't her mother. She couldn't just walk away. And Adam had known that all the time.

She tipped her head, finding his lips with hers, and her kiss was answered immediately by his, by the hunger in him that was deep inside her. The robe and towel were gone, and they were in the bedroom, the two of them, together in a way they never had been before. Without doubts and without fear, and just because they both loved each other.

Maggie went to him wholeheartedly, giving herself to him without reservation, without holding back anything, and Adam took her in the same way. He was over her, in her, filling her, and together they found a place where only the two of them could go. And they stayed there for what seemed a lifetime before the climax came and the descent to reality came with it.

They were tangled together, holding each other in the soft darkness. The rain was a mist, barely brushing the windows, and the cabin was warm and snug and perfect. Adam held his wife, relishing the oneness that was there, that had been there the first time and was back again. That sense of life being right. "You're okay with staying for the night?" he whispered against her bent head resting in the hollow of his shoulder.

She shifted, lifting herself on one elbow to look at him. "I'm still worried and I'm still going to be a mother who frets. I mean, there are five little lives to worry about." She dropped a kiss on his chest and felt him gasp at the contact. "I'm not perfect," she murmured, "but I'm okay. And the one thing I want right now is to make sure that you and I are okay."

He lifted a hand to touch her cheek. "Oh, we're okay, and we're okay if we go back now or if we stay."

"Then let's stay, and in the morning, we can call Grace and see how things are and see how she's holding up."

She traced the line of hair on his chest with her forefinger. "And if she's still sane and the babies are okay, what do you say we do what you wanted to begin with and stay for a few days?"

He covered her hand on his chest with his. "Do you mean it?"

"Oh, I mean it, I really mean it," she whispered and bent to kiss him. "Will you stay with me?" she asked.

"Oh, Maggie, forever," he said and drew her down to him, to show her that forever began right then.

Epilogue

Six months later

Maggie had wanted the birthday party for the quints to be quiet and just family, but Adam's father had insisted on giving it at the McCallum Multiple Birth Wing at the Maitland Maternity Clinic. A way to celebrate everything at once, all of the blessings in his life.

The guest list Maggie had, of just family, had expanded to include so many people she'd given up and let her father-in-law do it his way. The usually sterile cafeteria area was festooned with balloons, streamers and flowers, and three clowns made animals out of balloons and also painted faces.

The quiet halls were alive with adults and with the children who had been born there, the miracles of the clinic.

There were five cakes, three blue and two pink, on tables that looked like circus animals. Grandpa Jackson was carrying Douglas and his namesake, little Jackson. Grace had Julia, with Daniel toddling by her side, and Adam was just intercepting Gracie before she could put a hand in the nearest cake.

The quints didn't know what was going on, and they

didn't care. They loved the commotion, the attention and playing with the other kids. Maggie sat with her back against the wall, loving the five of them and their father.

"Hey there," someone said, and Maggie turned to find Annabelle Reardon—no, Beaumont now, the nurse who had been there when the babies had been born. "Isn't this fantastic?" Annabelle asked, looking around the transformed room.

"It's incredible," Maggie admitted. "Jackson thought it was a great idea, and I'm not up to fighting a McCallum man when he has his mind made up."

"I always knew you were smart," Annabelle said. "Can you believe it's been a whole year since those five little munchkins burst into this world?"

It seemed like a lifetime, yet as if it could have been just yesterday. "It's unbelievable," Maggie said. "I could never thank you and your husband enough for everything you did for all of us."

"Seeing you all here together is thanks enough, believe me. After everything you all went through, this is a certifiable miracle."

Maggie didn't argue. She nodded, her eyes burning at the memories of what they'd survived. They were still together, all of them. A real miracle. "You…did you get cake?"

"Cake? Did someone mention cake?" Zachary Beaumont was there, looking decidedly unlike a doctor. He came up behind his wife, hugging her to him and smiling as widely as Annabelle. "I love cake."

Maggie motioned to the five cakes. "Choose your color and go for it."

"Oh, I will," he said on a soft chuckle. "How about you, Annabelle? Cake? Or do you think you can keep it down?"

"None for me," she said.

"Okay, I'll be right back," Zach said and strode in the direction of the cake table.

Maggie looked at Annabelle, and something struck her. "You're sick?"

Annabelle blushed but looked incredibly healthy. "Oh, no. I'm fine."

"But he asked if you could..." She looked at Annabelle then, really looked at her. She was glowing. She had that look, and Maggie's eyes widened. "You're...you and Doctor Beaumont, you're expecting, aren't you?"

The blush deepened, and Annabelle lowered her voice. "We aren't making an announcement just yet. It's too early. I'm only six weeks along. We didn't think this would happen." She smiled a bit uncertainly. "It's almost too good to be true, you know what I mean?"

"I sure do," Maggie said, and hugged her. "This is so terrific. So...so..."

"It's a miracle, just like your five," Annabelle said. "A miracle." Then Zach was back with a plate but without any cake.

"No cake until they sing 'Happy Birthday,'" he said. And Maggie saw the way he looked at his wife, the same way Adam had looked at her during the pregnancy. That mixture of joy and worry. Happiness and uncertainty.

"We should be singing that pretty soon," Maggie said, and knew she needed Adam right then. She needed to get close to him, to feel him near, to make that physical connection between them. She needed it constantly, as much as she needed to know the babies were okay. "I'll be right back," she murmured, and saw Adam going out the door with Gracie on his shoulders. She went after him, into the hallway, and by the time she caught up to them, he was talking to Ian Russell.

She hadn't seen Ian or his wife, Madeline, the fertility specialist who had been the first to tell them there were five babies on the way, for what seemed a very long time. She knew they'd married, and she knew that Adam and Ian kept in touch off and on, on a business level.

"Ian?" she said, reaching for Gracie to slip her off Adam's shoulders and hug her to her chest. Gracie felt wonderfully heavy in her arms, a terrific feel for a baby who had felt so tiny and insubstantial for so long. But Gracie had other ideas, squirming until Maggie put her down.

"Maggie, I was just talking to your husband here about how you deal with having five babies. I think you're both miracle workers to get through it."

Maggie watched Gracie toddle toward Grace's husband, Douglas, in the doorway. The elderly man held out his arms, and she went right to him, then Maggie knew Gracie was safe and turned to Ian and her husband. She sought and found Adam's hand, holding it tightly and loving the way he held her. "No, we're just doing this day by day and figuring it out as we go along." She smiled. "Speaking of babies, I heard from someone that you and Madeline are expecting. Congratulations."

"I'll take a double dose of that," he said with a grin.

"Double?"

"As in twins."

"Oh, my gosh," Maggie gasped. "That's fantastic!"

"Pretty darn wonderful," Madeline said as she came up to them and very naturally slipped into her husband's hold.

That glow Maggie had seen in Annabelle was there a hundredfold in Madeline, along with the soft swelling of her stomach under the loose blue top she was wearing with black leggings. The woman looked wonderful with no makeup and her hair loose and curly.

"I was just getting some advice from these two," Ian said. "About how to deal with more than one baby coming into our lives."

"Oh, we can use all the advice we can get."

Adam let go of Maggie just long enough to change from holding her hand to putting his arm around her shoulders and pulling her against his side. "There is one thing you two should know, the most important thing," Adam said. "Don't ever lose each other in the middle of all the craziness."

Maggie could barely breathe for a second, remembering how close they'd come to doing that very thing themselves. "The two of you are the core of the family," she whispered. "And it's too easy to forget the most important things in this life."

"Good advice," Ian murmured, and she could see his hold on Maddie tightening just a bit. "Thanks for everything."

"No problem," Adam said, and glanced at Maggie.

She saw something in his eyes, something that made her look at Madeline and Ian and say, "I'm sorry, I came out here to talk to Adam."

"No problem," Ian said. "I'm sure you two don't get enough time together."

"We're working on it," Adam said.

Maggie waited until Ian and Madeline were out of earshot, then she turned to her husband. "What's wrong?"

He pulled her with him down the hall and into a quiet corner, never letting go of her. "I just keep thinking what could have happened to us, and instead, we're here and we're whole." He exhaled. "I need you, Maggie."

She went closer, circling his neck with her arms. "Your

timing isn't very good, is it? We're sort of committed to this party, you know?''

"Oh, I know, and I don't want to miss any of it. Not a minute of it." He kissed her, a lingering caress that drew at her soul and made a promise of things to come. "But after it's over—" he breathed roughly as he drew back away "—afterward, Grace and Douglas and my dad agreed to take care of the birthday kids for a few hours.''

"Oh, my, this sounds interesting," Maggie murmured. "And what exactly did you have in mind?"

"I'm open to anything you can come up with."

"Don't be so sure about that," she whispered.

"In an hour we can leave," he said. "Right after the cake and the presents." He exhaled roughly. "But right now we need to get back to the party."

She didn't want to let go, not yet, but she felt something at her legs, a tiny body pushing between the two of them, and she looked at little Jackson. He had chocolate cake all over his face and hands, and now that cake was all over the legs of Adam's pants and the pale ivory skirt of her dress. "You little dickens," Maggie said with a laugh, scooping him up, and when he giggled he showed an impressive number of teeth, the most of any of the quints.

"Let's go to the party," Maggie said, looking at Adam. "Shall we?"

"Absolutely," he answered, and they went together into the party room.

Everyone was there, and Jackson McCallum stood in the middle of everything. He held up a hand to silence the partygoers. "Everyone. Can I have your attention?"

The guests turned to him, and as Adam put his arm around Maggie, his dad, in a blue sports shirt with more than his share of chocolate cake smeared on it, looked around and smiled.

"What a day," he pronounced. "The birthday of my grandchildren, this place thriving and life itself! It was all worth it. A real labor of love!"

As he broke into a chorus of "Happy Birthday" and the others joined in, Adam looked at Maggie and leaned close enough so only she could hear him.

"Yes, it was worth everything."

This Mother's Day Give Your Mom A Royal Treat

Win a fabulous one-week vacation in Puerto Rico for you and your mother at the luxurious Inter-Continental San Juan Resort & Casino. The prize includes round trip airfare for two, breakfast daily and a mother and daughter day of beauty at the beachfront hotel's spa.

INTER·CONTINENTAL
San Juan
RESORT & CASINO

Here's all you have to do:

Tell us in 100 words or less how your mother helped with the romance in your life. It may be a story about your engagement, wedding or those boyfriends when you were a teenager or any other romantic advice from your mother. The entry will be judged based on its originality, emotionally compelling nature and sincerity. See official rules on following page.

Send your entry to:
Mother's Day Contest

In Canada	**In U.S.A.**
P.O. Box 637	P.O. Box 9076
Fort Erie, Ontario	3010 Walden Ave.
L2A 5X3	Buffalo, NY
	14269-9076

Or enter online at www.eHarlequin.com

All entries must be postmarked by April 1, 2002.
Winner will be announced May 1, 2002. Contest open to
Canadian and U.S. residents who are 18 years of age and older.
No purchase necessary to enter. Void where prohibited.

PRROY

**Meet the Randall brothers...four sexy bachelor brothers
who are about to find four beautiful brides!**

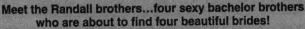

by bestselling author

Judy Christenberry

In preparation for the long, cold Wyoming winter, the
eldest Randall brother seeks to find wives for his four
single rancher brothers...and the resulting matchmaking is
full of surprises! Containing the first two full-length novels
in Judy's famous *4 Brides for 4 Brothers* miniseries,
this collection will bring you into the lives, and loves,
of the delightfully engaging Randall family.

Look for WYOMING WINTER in March 2002.

And in May 2002 look for SUMMER SKIES,
containing the last two Randall stories.

HARLEQUIN®

Makes any time special ®

Visit us at www.eHarlequin.com

PHWW